Monster INK Publishing
Presents

FUELED

BY

REVENGE 2

BB. HUGHLEY

CONTENTS

JAXSYN
JAXSYN
MESSIAH
ZIONNA
JAXSYN

Jaxsyn

I looked over at the clock on my dresser and it was 5:49 am. I didn't know why Gizmo was knocking on my bedroom door, but I got up anyway.

"What?" I opened the door and he stormed past me.

Close that," he pointed to the door. Now put her down and come holla at me in this bathroom," he went in there and leaned against the sink. For some reason unknown to me, I did what he said.

As soon as I got to the bathroom, he snatched me up and shook me hard.

"I want you to wake the fuck up and shake this shit off. This shit ain't you, my nigga. I watched you torture three muthafuckas for hours without flinching or blinking an eye. It's a fuckin beast inside of you and this is the time to unleash that bitch. This is the time to let loose," he punched me in my chest so hard he took my breath away. "These hoe ass niggas came in y'all fuckin' crib and got your fuckin' babies and you're held up in this bitch like he's just going to bring them the fuck back. You're smarter than this Jaxsyn, it's time to wake the fuck up, and I mean now. Ain't no bitch in yo' blood. I've seen your heart and it can turn black and cold as ice. I need that muthafucka to surface right the fuck now. Your kids need you and yo' nigga is breaking the fuck down mentally. He can only take so much B, so step the fuck up like I know you can so we

can get y'all shit back in order. The babies need to be home in they fuckin' bed and they need us all to make that shit happen," he turned me toward the mirror. "Look at you. You look mad crazy Ma and everybody's fuckin worried that you're going to off your fuckin self in this bitch any day now. Hop the fuck in that got damn shower and come watch this footage with me. You have an eye and ear for this shit. Listen to everything this nigga says and everything the nigga don't say. Watch how he moves and pay attention to every got damn thing going on around him. Take your emotions out of it for a minute and really pay attention Jaxsyn. Give the baby to Sih and meet me in the basement after your shower. He misses her and it's some real hoe ass shit to keep her from him under the fuckin circumstances. You already fuckin' know that though, so I shouldn't have even had to say that shit bro. Real spit," he pushed past me hard as hell, knocking me into the counter, and I was at a loss for words. I stared at myself in the mirror and he was one hundred percent right across the board. I had completely fuckin' lost it and got caught up in my grief. Sih was an afterthought to me for the last few days even though he's the only one in the world that knew how I was feeling. We were in this together and I was fuckin' up.

I turned on the shower and hopped in. I let the hot water beat down on my back as I cried, and the water washed my tears away. I washed myself thoroughly because it had been days and then got out. Slipping into my black jogging suit with my black Timbs and putting my hair in a messy bun, had me feeling a little better and I damn sure smelled better.

Messiah was sitting on the couch with his head laid back and his fitted over his face. I placed Jeniah on his chest and he jumped. He moved his hat and looked down at her. Tears welled up in his eyes and I kissed his forehead. I was wrong for keeping her away from him and I felt like shit. I walked away without saying a word and I went to the basement with Gizmo. I guess the cleaners had come to the house because there was no sign of Tabitha anywhere.

I put the DVD in and for well over two hours, me and Gizmo picked the video apart inch by inch.

"Wait. Go back, go back," I stopped him, and he rewound it.

"Abra Ca Muthafuckin Dabra nigga," I had heard that shit somewhere, but I couldn't place it. I took the remote from Giz and kept rewinding it over and over until it hit me like a ton of fuckin bricks.

"Ollie," I stood up. "He fuckin knows Ollie. Ollie is the connection. I told you Ollie was the small fish, and this is the shark we've been looking for."

"My nigga. I knew it was in you," he pushed me playfully.

"Remember when we finally found Ollie and that nigga was talking shit to him and-"

"Ollie came out with the burner and said the same shit. Ol' boy didn't think he was strapped."

"Exactly," I nodded my head. "Now we just need to know how he's connected to him."

"I'm on it cuz. I told you it was a fuckin beast in there. This is guerilla warfare Baby, and we need you present," he hugged me and ran upstairs. I followed behind him and I felt slightly better that we were one step closer. He said something to Messiah and left out the door.

"What did y'all find?" Messiah looked over at me and his tone was dry.

"Hopefully a connection," I shrugged, and he directed his attention back to Jeniah. "I'm sorry for-"

"Stop Jaxsyn," he stroked Jeniah's face as she slept peacefully in his arms. "We're not about to fight and argue because we're both hurting and what's happened has taken a toll on us both. This shit is enough to drive anyone insane. Let's just leave it at that."

"I love you."

7

"I love you too Baby," he looked back towards me and I walked over to him. I sat down and kissed him deeply. We shared a moment that we both needed and tears rolled down both of our faces.

"I don't want you to suffer through this alone Ma."

"I know. I had a moment but I'm back," I kissed him again and then looked at our sleeping daughter. "I swear I'm back."

"Good. We have to find these muthafuckas and make them pay. I have a few more of my cousins coming out here because I don't trust none of these muthafuckas now. None."

"I'm ready for whatever will get our kids back safe and sound," I laid in his arms and I could feel his anger radiating off of him. Clearly this nigga had a beast inside of him too. You don't fuck with people kids. The line had been crossed and we were war ready.

Messiah

Jax and I stayed up all night thinking of how this shit could play out and what moves we needed to make. We agreed that Jeniah had to go somewhere safe and the safest place for her was with my people in New York. We told Zionna we needed her to hold us down and take her out there with my cousin Shawn. We could tell she was nervous, but we needed this and she knew it.

I held Jaxsyn in my arms as we watched my cousin and her sister drive away with the only baby that we had left. My heart was in a chokehold and stomach was in knots for both of us, but it was nothing else that we could do. I had to protect my baby girl and I know my fam wouldn't let a hair on her head get harmed. For the first time in a long time, I had no doubt in my mind that we made the right decision.

"Let's get in here and map this shit out ma. Gizmo said he has more information," I wiped her face and she nodded. My whole living room was filled with family and she had no idea when I said they were coming that it was going to be this many. It was nineteen of my closest cousins and they were all ready for whatever, whenever.

"Thanks to Jaxsyn I know who the fuck we're looking for." Gizmo put his picture in the middle of our living room table and my cousin Fresh spoke up first.

"I know this muthafucka," he rubbed his head. "His name is Dominic. They call him Gato which is cat in Spanish. He's the leader of the Vargas Cartel and he's notorious for being vicious but he plays with his prey which is why they call the nigga Gato. This nigga is heavily guarded, but he goes rogue every now and then."

"Cartel? How the fuck did we cross paths with this muthafucka?" I looked at Gizmo.

"Stepped on his toes one too many times, I'm guessing. Apparently, he was fuckin your girl, Mariah behind your back for years. We popped that bitch then we killed his little brother Ollie for killing Nashon. His cousin Rodney was The Knight that y'all caught trying steal from y'all and you and Nash handled his ass too. I'm assuming Tone knew Ollie through him coming around with Dominic while he was fuckin' Mariah."

"Wow. So, were these niggas coming for us through that nigga Rodney or was that some fluke shit?"

"I'm still working on that, but it seems like it was all a part of a plan. This couldn't be that much of a coincidence," I rubbed my hands over my face and the reality of my actions hit me all at once. My kids were kidnapped and caught in the middle of my bullshit. Now they're telling me that not only does this lunatic that has my babies have cartel connections, but this shit may be even deeper than we originally thought. I'd killed that nigga Rodney almost two years ago and now this shit is coming back at me. They were trying to infiltrate our shit all the way back then. I knew that shit felt bigger at the time, but I couldn't figure that shit out and today I wasn't any closer.

"The shit gets a little worse, cuz." Gizmo looked at both me and Jaxsyn.

"Nigga," I shook my head.

"Look who he passed the kids to on the video," he sat down the blown up still frame from the video. I couldn't believe my eyes and Jaxsyn looked like she was about to throw up.

"Sandy?" Tears rolled down her face. "That's how the nigga knows so much about us. He could go after anybody next to hurt us even more," she took her phone out and called Zionna.

"Please answer the phone," Jaxsyn paced.

"Hello."

"Yeah."

"Have you talked to Sandy?"

"Not in a few days."

"Good. This bitch was with him when he took the kids Z."

"What?" She yelled into the phone.

"Yeah. Do not tell her anything. She's probably feeding this nigga all kinds of information on us."

"Who the fuck is he and why would she be helping him do some shit like this?"

"Somebody named Dominic and I don't know. Drugs, money, her granddaughter that she didn't want me to have in the first place. Who fuckin knows with her?"

"Let me talk to her," I snatched the phone out of Jax's hand. "Sis, call her. See if she gives you any information. Y'all say she likes to run her mouth, so make her believe that you're on your way back to Arizona and you got into an argument with Jaxsyn. Call her now on the three way."

"Can you pull over?" She asked my cousin Shawn. "I have to get out of the car Messiah. Jeniah has been crying since we left."

"Okay," she briefly paused and then I heard the phone ringing.

"Hello."

"Hey ma."

"Hey baby. Where are you?"

"On my way back to Arizona. You know I went on that vacation with Jaxsyn and her sisters."

"Did that bitch treat you right or she was actin' funny like I told you she would?"

"Actin' funny. You were right about her once again and I shouldn't have gone. Where are you?"

"That dusty bitch doesn't know any better. Look at who raised her. I told you she's not family."

"You were right too. Where you at?"

"You wouldn't believe me if I told you," she laughed.

"Try me."

"Arizona."

"Did you come to visit me?"

"Not really, but I do have a surprise for you if you can keep a secret. Hold on." We could hear her walking and then the door closed. "Hello."

"Yeah. What's the secret?"

"I can get your baby back from Jaxsyn if you still want her."

"I definitely want her. You know she belongs with family, right?"

"Right. The light bulb finally fuckin' came on for you girl. She's ours. Our blood. Not that fake ass wanna be sister." Sandy whispered and we all listened on speakerphone.

"So how are you going to get her back? I signed her over ma."

"Fuck them papers, girl. I got her already, but you can't say shit, Z. Not a fuckin' word bitch. This nigga crazy as hell. I mean the real kind of crazy Z, so just keep your mouth shut and I got us. Shit, I think he killed Kabrina the other day, so the nigga ain't nothin' to be played with. Don't say shit," I looked over at Jaxsyn and she had a blank expression on her face.

"What?"

"Yeah. I'll explain all that lil shit later but listen to this, he says I can keep her if I do what I have to do. He wants Jaxsyn and her baby daddy dead so if I give him what he need, he said I can keep her."

"Good." Zionna's whole demeanor had changed, and I hoped that Sandy didn't pick up on it because we all started to look around at each other.

"Alright baby. I'll be back in Detroit tonight. He wants us to show him where Jax's baby daddy grandmother lives and then yo' no good ass daddy is after that. Once that's done, I can take the baby and go."

"So, should I stay in Detroit and wait for y'all?"

"Yeah. Just stay there and meet me at my house. That way we can all go back to Arizona together as a family."

"Okay. Bet."

She hung up and Zionna started crying.

"Tell Shawn to bring y'all back," I hung up and held Jaxsyn. My baby was suffering, and it was all coming at her from different angles. I swear I hope her mother is still alive and this nigga didn't do that shit.

"We have to get granny out of that house. This nigga is coming for straight blood and he's not stopping." My cousin James said through gritted teeth.

"Take my family and your family to the house in the woods. We know for a fact no one knows about it but us, so they'll be safe there." Jaxsyn wiped her face and stood up. "Half of us go post up at my dad's and the other half of us go post up and Granny Knights house. We don't know if he has the babies with him, but we have to hit him before he hits us again and this is the only way. What we do know is that he's in Arizona, so we have the upper hand right now. He's bold so he's going to want to be the first one out and we make our move from there. Did y'all hear her say he wants 'us' to show him. It's more people or another person. Ugh, this shit is crazy."

"Yeah, I heard that shit," I nodded. My head was pounding.

"Are we killing this nigga on sight or are we taking him for information." Fresh asked.

"Information. I need to find my children if he doesn't have them with him and from the sounds of all this, it's getting deeper. We need to eliminate everyone involved."

"Bet." Everyone started moving and I looked at Gizmo. He had a lot of confidence in Jaxsyn and now I see why. She was a leader and even I didn't mind following her plan. I looked around the room and I knew that I may lose some of these people tonight but unfortunately, I didn't have any other choice, my kids' lives were on the line.

"Oh," Jaxsyn said, and everyone stopped. "Can somebody please go check on my momma?"

"We got you Ma." One of my cousins said as they walked out, and I texted the address. I kissed her and we followed everyone else out of the door.

Jaxsyn

The coldness that Gizmo knew my heart held had surfaced and all I could think about was revenge. Revenge for Nash, revenge for my nigga going to jail and missing out on the first year of our children's lives, revenge for the betrayal that was lurking so close to us, revenge for Tabitha, revenge for how these bitches did my babies, revenge for turning our whole world upside down. I wanted Dominic's blood on my hands. I wanted him dead in the worst kind of way, but I needed him to suffer first. A quick death was too good for him.

This nigga took my kids from me and now he's probably killed my fuckin mother. She just got her shit together and was out here doing everything in her power to right her wrongs and this bitch ass nigga stole her from me. I couldn't even remember the last time I told her that I loved her, and it was bothering me. All she wanted was for me to call her momma and she never even got to hear me utter those words, but I swear I felt it. She really stepped up these last few years and I loved her ass so much for it.

I wiped the tears that fell just at the thought of what he took from me. He was walking around thinking shit was sweet, but I was willing to go to hell and back to avenge the people he stole from me and the shit he's put us through. Fuck his brothers' bitch ass, that hoe Mariah, and his shady ass cousin Rodney too. All they asses deserved what they got and he's next.

We couldn't give our families much information, but we made sure they knew it was imperative that they didn't use their phones for anything and that they stayed in The Spot which was the safest place for them at the moment. My daddy tried to give us a hard time because Rebecca was at

15

work, but I assured him that as soon as she turned her phone back on, we'll make sure she's brought to him. After about five more minutes of worrying he gave in and went with Messiah's cousins. He knew me well enough to know I wouldn't allow anything to happen to her.

When Zionna and Shawn got back we had him take her and Jeniah there too. We had to make sure that this shit played out like it was supposed to and we didn't lose anyone else.

"You ready for this Tink?" Messiah looked over at me while we sat across the street from his grandmother's house, and I nodded my head yes.

"I want this nigga dead, Baby."

"Me too." His eyes were dark and filled with hate.

"I can't believe our fuckin lives just changed this drastically."

"I know. We can't catch a fuckin' break," he shook his head.

"Not one. Nashon died and then everything went downhill. Sometimes I feel like I'm dreaming."

"This is a fuckin' nightmare Tink. A long ass fuckin' nightmare, and now we're going after Freddie Krueger," he looked across the street and we both peeped a van pulling up slowly. It rode past the house and we ducked all the way down. A few minutes later the same van pulled back around and parked in front of the house.

I said a silent prayer that we both make it out of this situation safely but also that Dominic was the one to step out. They sat there for about five minutes as we watched in silence and then my heart started pounding so loud that I thought Sih could hear it. There he was, in the flesh. The first fuckin one to step out just like I said he would. That was one of the first things that I peeped when I watched the footage from our home. He didn't have back up. Fresh said he's normally heavily guarded but it was only him and the person that he passed my babies to which we now know

16

was Sandy. He's cocky and think he's untouchable. Little did he know, we ain't to be fucked with and it was a group of nigga's waiting for him in the house.

Dominic finally slithered his snake ass out of the van and snuck around the back of the house. A few seconds later we saw the living room light come on and we knew his ass was caught. That was our cue. Me, Messiah, and two of his cousins snuck over to the van and peeped that he had a passenger. Messiah snatched the door open, and his cousin hit his ass one time and put that nigga to sleep. They carried him across the street and tossed him in the trunk while me and Sih crept around to the back of the van. We looked at each other before snatching both doors open at the same time. Never in a million years was I prepared for who was in the back with Sandy. Before I could even wrap my head around what the fuck was happening, Messiah raised his gun and she raised hers too. Sandy rocked my daughter back and forth with a smug smirk on her face.

"Rebecca?" Tears of confusion filled my eyes as both her and Sih squeezed the trigger at the same time!

Present

Jaxsyn

"Rebecca?"
"Mommy!"

Bang! Bang!

Two shots rang out and my heart dropped, but my mind, body, and soul were stuck in a trance. A split second ago you couldn't have paid me to believe what the fuck my eyes were seeing in this moment. Did Rebecca really betray me like this and help Dominic and Sandy kidnap my babies? What the hell was I missing? What the fuck did I ever do to her to deserve this kind of betrayal? Is my father in on this too? My siblings...

My mother could possibly be dead, and this bitch was a part of the scheme the whole damn time. Possibly my whole family... The people nearest and dearest to me were fuckin' snakes! Dominic didn't even need Sandy when he had Rebecca, who literally knows everything about me. She's been my shoulder to cry on and a listening ear my entire life. She knows more about me than either one of my biological parents.

The screams coming from behind me snatched me out of the trance I had slipped into and I turned around. Alyssa was shaking like a leaf and screaming at the top of her lungs. I turned back around, and Sandy's brain matter was splattered all over the van and Rebecca, but the only thing I gave a fuck about was my daughter that was still in Sandy's arms. As death came to collect, her body went limp, and I needed my daughter away from all of this dysfunction.

"Jaxsyn… Mommy?" Alyssa's voice trembled as I held my gun aimed directly at Rebecca's head. She wasn't about this life that she was pretending to be about but I damn sure was. Messiah's gun was the only one smoking which means she pulled her gun and didn't use that bitch. That was mistake number two, number one was fuckin' with my children. I let my bullets fly and her body jerked but Messiah knocked my arm down.

"Noooo!" Alyssa started running towards us.

"Baby no. Nevaeh is right there." Both of their actions gave Rebecca the moment she needed to get away and she seized the opportunity. She scurried to the front of the van and hopped into the driver's seat. Messiah and I dove towards the back of the van at the same time as if our brains were synced, and I snatched my baby out of Sandy's arms just in the nick of time. Rebecca hit the gas hard as fuck and burned-out making Sandy's limp body roll around in the back of the van.

"Jaxsyn please tell me what's happening? Please tell me what's going on. Mrs. Knight made you a pot of chicken noodle soup and baked you a German chocolate cake because Zionna said you were sick and then I get here to pick it up and… and," she broke down crying hysterically. As much as I wanted to give a fuck, I couldn't. In mere seconds, my heart had turned cold towards the people that I would have died for once upon a time. I didn't know if the tears drenching her face were a part of the plot that had just thickened or not, but I was done giving muthafuckas the benefit of doubt. I backed away from her and looked down at my baby girl who was smiling up at me and her father, bringing us to an overwhelming moment. We both cried for ourselves, her, and the situation we still faced.

"Boo boo, Daddy?" She reached over and wiped the tears from his face.

"Nah Princess, Daddy's good." He leaned down placing kisses all over her face and then mine. We looked at each other and we knew shit had just went left and we couldn't fully enjoy this moment because Junior was still missing, we still hadn't heard back from his cousins about Kabrina, and now Dominic was more of a threat to us than ever before. With Rebecca by his side there was no limit to the damage he could cause in our life. This whole scene and the reality of this betrayal had me physically ill.

"Aye cuz, we about to head in here." Haze and Wally, his two cousins that had been with us said from the lawn just as gun shots started going off inside of their granny's house. We all ducked, and Messiah covered Nevaeh and I as he pushed us towards the car we came in.

"Don't leave me." Alyssa screamed as she followed.

"No." I stopped her dead in her tracks before she hopped into my car. "I can't have you around my baby. Go back to your car and get out of here."

"What?" She looked at me with confusion written deep within her expression. Under normal circumstances, that look would have gotten her anything she wanted from me. Not today. There is literally no one on this planet more important than my children, and when that line was crossed, everything inside of me changed. Knowing that muthafuckas I've known my whole life had a hand in harming and kidnapping my children did something vicious to my spirit. I eyed her with the same disgust I'd eyed her mother with just moments ago and Messiah stepped in between us.

"Get in this car with my daughter and drive off Jaxsyn. We don't have time for this shit."

"Hell no. Get in this car with us Sih. Please. Don't do this." I grabbed his hand, and he kissed the back of mine.

"I have to go in here and see what the fuck is going on baby. I can't let them kill this nigga without finding out where our son is first and if the situation just went left like it did out here, I can't let my fam handle it alone."

"Sih, I need you. *We* need you. I'm not fuckin' losing you. I've almost--" He kissed me and then stared deeply into my eyes.

"Get in the fuckin' car like I just told you to do baby. I'm not repeating myself again. If I'm not back in ten minutes take my daughter to safety Jaxsyn. Call Shawn from the burner and tell him what just went down and then tell him you need to talk to your pops. We need to know what the fuck is going on and how deep this shit goes. Then have Shawn call Fresh to check on what they found at Kabrina's house." He kissed Nevaeh several times and then kissed me. "Ten minutes baby. I love y'all." He turned around to Alyssa with his gun pointed straight at her head. Fear drained the color from her face, and she started shaking even more than she already was. "I love you like blood Lyss, I swear I do but if you had anything to do with any of this shit, I'll put a bullet in your head quicker than I just did Sandy. You can play with your life if you want to, and you'll end up unidentifiable, in a fuckin' ditch next to your mother." His words dripped venom and she cried silent tears. "Go get in the car." He looked back at me and then ran across the street. I stared at my little sister for a brief moment before we both hopped in the car and I told her to lay her seat back.

"Jax please tell me what's going on. None of this makes sense. I came for a fuckin' get well soon package because she didn't want to drive it across town. Like, this is just... I just don't know..." I rocked my baby and looked at her heavy eyes start to close. I prayed this day would come and it felt so surreal to have her back in my arms again.

"Your mother is a snake that I regret trusting." I kissed Nevaeh's head. "I wasn't sick, I was having a mental breakdown. Someone kidnapped her and Junior and killed Tabitha the day we got back from our vacation." She gasped but I never looked her way. I had obviously been around a bunch of fuckin' actresses so I wasn't moved by her tears or sound effects in the least bit. "Tonight, was the night that we were going to get at the guy Dominic that did all of this shit, and Sandy, who we just found out was working with him. Much to our surprise, Rebecca was in the back of the van with Sandy and working with this Dominic person as well."

"Wait, what? How? Why? Like, we've all seen her with her grand babies Jax. This doesn't make any sense. She loves them. Heck, she loves you." I turned around and her face was soaked in fresh tears.

"Yeah, well, we both just saw her in the back of the van that my kidnapped daughter was in with the person that we found out from, and the person that did it was driving. We also saw her pull a gun on me and my fiancé too, right? We also saw her snake ass scurry to the front of the same van and burn out without an explanation too, right?" I snapped and she got quiet. "Right." I rolled my eyes. "That bitch wasn't cuffed, scared of Dominic, or being held against her will in any way." I pulled my phone out and called Shawn. I was over talking to Alyssa.

"Hey Shawn, it's Jax." I discreetly told him about my stepmother's slithering ass and then asked him to put my father on the phone.

"Man, this shit is crazy. Giz say he got some shit he needs to holla at y'all about too. I just hit his line and shit is quiet at yo' people house, but now we know why."

"Exactly." I exhaled deeply just thinking about everything that was happening.

"Hold on, let me get this nigga for you." I kissed all over my daughter's face as I watched Grandma Knight's house like a hawk and waited for my dad to get his ass on this phone. Time seemed like it was going slow as molasses, or it had just completely stopped.

"Hello." I put the phone on speakerphone.

"Your wife is a snake. Are you one too?" I wasn't in the mood to bullshit around and being discreet was no longer on the table. When I heard his voice, I became more pissed.

"Excuse me?"

"I want an answer! Rebecca helped abduct my children and I caught her red handed so don't even try to feed me no bullshit. Did you know about her working with Dominic?"

"Who is Dominic, and what are you even talking about Jaxsyn?" He seemed annoyed which pissed me off even more.

"My children! That's what I'm talking about!" I screamed causing Alyssa and Nevaeh to jump. I didn't mean to scare my baby after everything she's been through, but my emotions were running wild, and I felt like my intelligence was being toyed with. I couldn't control my anger or the tears that started to fall. The people closest to me had betrayed a trust that I thought was unbreakable. They'd smiled in my face at family functions and plotted against me at the same time.

"Jeniah is right here in my arms baby. Where's--"

"Someone took them right out of our home, and we didn't want to scare everyone, plus I kind of had a breakdown." I started giving him the cliff notes version of what'd transpired so far. Alyssa still hadn't stopped crying or shaking. "Daddy, did you know? Please tell me you didn't know. Kabrina might be dead because of all of this, and if you--" More shots rang out in the house and then people started running out of the front door yelling something. I dropped the phone and reached for the door handle.

"Jax no! Sih said."

BOOM! An explosion went off in the house and the car shook like we were in an earthquake. I started screaming which made my baby start crying and Alyssa started her theatrics again too.

Jaxsyn… Jax… Jax say something… Jax what was that noise… My father was calling out to me, but I couldn't believe what the fuck I had just witnessed. I couldn't lose Messiah after everything we've been through. I just couldn't. I hopped out of the car without thinking and ran toward the burning house with my baby on my hip and my sister on my heels. People were laid out everywhere, coughing and gasping for air. Now that we were closer, I could see it was much worse than I thought. The roof collapsed and only a small portion of the house was still standing. The smoke was thick as hell and getting thicker by the second. I buried my baby's face in my shirt and kept moving forward.

"Messiah!" I yelled out and got no response.

"Messiah!" Lyss called out to him.

"Sih, baby please answer me! Siiiih!" I had my crying daughter in my left arm, but my right hand was locked and loaded with my Glock. I didn't know what to expect as we crept up, but we all had to make it through this night. "Messiah!"

"He's back here Jax." I heard Solo's voice and raised my gun. We purposely didn't tell any Knight's because we didn't know who the fuck we could trust.

"Get away from him." I said with the purest form of hate in my heart. Solo had two other Knight's with him, and I was ready to risk it all to make sure my man didn't meet his demise at their hands. I heard sirens in the distance, but I didn't give a damn. I wasn't leaving from this spot without Messiah.

24

"Jax, it's me, Solo." They all raised their hands and backed away from Sih when they saw I wasn't lowering my weapon.

"How did you know we were here?"

"Gizmo. He knew we could be trusted, and he told us what was going down. He told us to hang back, but we saw some niggas sneaking through the alley to come through the house from the backyard. By the time we ran down here, one of the niggas fired a fuckin' rocket launcher at the house. I don't know how they found out in the house, but right before he let that bitch rip, they all started running out the front door yelling for everyone to get down."

"Sih!" I called out to him and he wasn't moving.

"Oh my God." Lyss covered her mouth as she stood next to me but damn near in the same skin ass me. I'm almost positive we were breathing the same air she was so close.

"We gotta get him to Doc, sis. He got some kind of metal shavings, or some shit lodged into his chest. I don't know how deep it is, but he's bleeding, and I think the impact knocked him out."

"Baby." I ran to him and he was out cold and bleeding like Solo said.

"I would never in my life go against the grain, Jax. Ever. Y'all can trust me and *right now*, I need that to happen." He snatched me up so hard I almost dropped Nevaeh and my gun. Lyss started swinging on him immediately.

"Let her go!" He ignored her hits and screams.

"Grab Sih!" He barked at Glen and Jason. "Now niggas!" He yelled and started running as he damn near dragged me. I hadn't noticed the car that was coming through the alley speeding. He started yelling for all of Sih's cousins to run. They were still helping each other up, dusting themselves off, and choking from the smoke in the air, on the front lawn. They instantly started pulling their weapons back out and all hell broke loose. Gun fire was coming from every direction and the police sirens that were in the distance just moments ago were drawing nearer. It sounded like a damn war zone and my heart was pounding out of my chest. Solo kept running until we were all at the car. They laid Sih across the backseat and he said he would text me the address to take him to. Shit was happening so fast I pulled off with my daughter still in my lap. I snatched the seatbelt towards us and Lyss snapped it in as I did a hundred miles per hour through a residential neighborhood. I had to get the fuck on, and I had to do it quick. All I could do is pray that his cousins would make it through that shit that had just popped off, but I had to get my man out of there and I wasn't stopping until I got him to whoever "Doc" is.

Rebecca Blackwell

"I'm so sorry Rebecca." Brian bent down in front of me as my heart broke into pieces. My family had disowned me over this man. I haven't talked to them in years because they didn't approve of him. Now he's sitting me down for the second time in less than six months, telling me about another trashy whore he's gotten pregnant. Two damn kids on the way and he's in front of me high as a kite. The nerve.

Drugs had turned our lives upside down within the last couple of years. He's always dabbled in coke, even in college. It was recreationally acceptable, and everyone was experimenting. Never in a million years did I think he would become addicted, obviously I was wrong. He's managed to take this family down a path of destruction that I never saw coming our way. I was sure we had hit rock bottom months ago, but he found a way to lower us even beyond that point. He didn't even consider our boys and how this would confuse and affect them. It's all about Brian and what his drug induced mind tells him to do.

"Two different women Brian?" My hand rested on my chest as I panted and tried my hardest to catch my breath. "Two!"

"All I can do is apologize Bec. Sandy was never supposed to get pregnant. Ever! I swear to God it was a mistake."

I stopped and looked at him like he had lost his fucking mind, because he had to have lost it to say something like that to me. Was he serious? "And the other trashy bitch was Brian?" Did he even realize what he had just said to me? His new wife.

"That's not what I... I only meant... I was just saying that--"

"Oh God. Brian no. You love her?" I snatched my hand away from him. "You love this woman, and this doesn't have a damn thing to do with drugs. You weren't high, you were willing."

"Becca."

"NO!" I yelled and he jumped. I had never raised my voice at him before or anyone else, but this was my breaking point. He had finally pushed me too far. Sure, we may not have had an ideal beginning, but he told me he was in this with me, when we decided to get married a few months ago. We still hadn't even told anyone that we went to Ohio to elope and now he's telling me he has two motherfucking kids on the way by whores. As if that wasn't enough, he chose to drive the dagger into my heart a little deeper by standing in front of me displaying his love for one of them. I could see it written all over his face. He couldn't hide his true feelings if he tried, which he didn't, and it hurt. "Don't you dare Becca me, Brian. I'm home every goddamn night with our boys while you go out into the ghetto doing drugs and plowing women that I can smell on you when you get home. You're hanging with your cousins so much that you've missed three of Dawson's games this year. THREE Brian! My whole family hates me because of you but I still chose you anyway. I literally have no friends since you decided to move me from Howell down here to Bloomfield Hills, where I know absolutely no one outside of your family. The same family that believes I trapped you and disrespects me every time I come around. I sacrificed everything for us Brian." I shook my head. "Your very existence disgusts me right now. I want you out of my home." I stormed out of the room and he followed me.

"It's not what you think Rebecca, please allow me to explain." Words were coming from his mouth, but I *know what I saw on his face and he couldn't feed me a lie good enough to change what I knew in my heart.*

"Oh, okay, so there's really an explanation for two goddamn children outside of our brand-new marriage? A marriage that you agreed to. A marriage that you said you would respect no matter how we started out or what people think about us. Like I said, you seriously disgust me. You really do." We stared at each other and I couldn't stop shaking my head. When I said I was disgusted, I meant it with every fiber of my being. I went upstairs and started packing both of my son's clothes since realistically my husband wasn't going to leave. Brian stood in the doorway begging me to reconsider leaving as my heart was pounding inside of my chest with every single word he spoke. Rage coursed through my veins like never before, but I loved my husband, and I never wanted this to be us. I never wanted my parents to be right, but they were. They told me that he would eventually leave me for some black bitch that could give him something that I couldn't. I didn't know what that "something" was, but obviously he found it in one of his whores and the shit hurt like hell.

"Be honest Brian, do you love this woman?" I stopped packing and turned around to face him. I knew the answer, but stupidly I held my breath and waited for him to say it out loud. He put his head down and a gut-wrenching pain shot through my soul.

"I do."

I couldn't stop the tears from falling even if I wanted to. "How could you do this to me when I gave up everything for you? Everything Brian. I haven't laid eyes on my family in years. They don't even know our boys. Do you know how painful it is for your own parents to disown you because of who you love only for them to be right in the end?"

"Rebecca this has nothing to do with how amazing you are. I fucked up. I'm a flawed man that fucked up,

baby. Please let me make this right. I'll do whatever it takes. I'll get help. I'll cater to your every need. I'll never miss another one of the boy's games. I'll be home every night for dinner. Just don't leave me baby. We have to think about our children. I want our boys to have a real family. That was the agreement and I promise I'm going to straighten the fuck up and give them that." He pulled me into his arms. It's his charm that got me from the beginning. He'd always been smooth, and his penis is like nothing I've ever experienced before. The same penis that I thought was solely mine... "Please, baby." He started kissing on my neck as his hands caressed my lower back, and I cried harder on his shoulder. I didn't want him to feel this good. I didn't want all those old feelings to come rushing back to me. I wanted to be mad as hell in this moment, I wanted to hate him for hurting me, but the more he touched me, the more I fell under his spell. "I'm sorry Bec," he whispered, as he picked me up and carried me out of our boy's room and into ours. "Let me get us back on track baby." He laid me down and looked deep into my eyes. "I fucked up and I'm man enough to admit that, but I care about this family enough to change. Let me prove it baby." He pushed himself deep inside of me and I gasped for air. Each stroke drove me crazy and deeper in love with my husband. I knew by the time I started screaming his name and shaking from pleasure that I would be helping him raise two children that weren't my own.

****

Depression crept into my world without a single warning. Months of worrying about what Brian was doing whenever he left home, who he was with, what they were doing, and how I was going to accept outside children was weighing heavy on me. I helped people manage their feelings, thoughts, and emotions, on a daily basis but I

30

couldn't manage my own. I couldn't get a handle on anything I was feeling, or the constant mood swings I was thrown into without notice. Brian didn't just love this woman who I found out was also doing drugs like him and the first woman he told me about, but he was actually in love with her. What they shared was deep and kept me up crying many nights, driving me further into the deepest darkest crevices of my mind.

I listened to him talk to her on the speaker phone in his car one night while he was parked in our garage. His window was rolled down while he was smoking weed. I've always hated having that smell lingering in our home so he would go smoke outside. A few times I heard him talking but didn't pay it any attention until I heard a female's voice days prior. I knew it wasn't one of his cousins because of the tone in her voice but he hung up before I could hear what was being said. I stalked that garage door for days before I caught him. They say when you go seeking you shall find... and I found...

"Bri Bri we have our baby girl on the way. We have to get our shit together for her baby. You were high as fuck yesterday and my daughter better not come out fucked up."

"I'm trying baby. This shit is so hard Bri, but I don't want anything to be wrong with our princess either. I love her already."

"I love her too, Beautiful. I hope she comes out looking just like you, baby."

"I hope all this ass skips a generation because she's going to have us in jail trying to keep the boys away."

"You already know, because I can't keep my hands off of you, never could."

"And I love when they on me handsome. I love you so much Bri and I swear I'm going to do better for her and us."

"I love you more baby. Let me get in this house. I'll see you in the morning. Stay out them fuckin' streets Kabrina and away from Sandy's nothin' ass."

"I should be saying that to you."

"Don't start that stupid shit. Who has my heart?"

Pregnant pause… no pun intended. "Me." They said their goodbyes with a couple more I love you's and my heart shattered inside of my chest. I had never felt heartbreak so deeply in my life. The tone in which he spoke to her and the flow of their conversation was nothing like anything we've ever experienced together. I wondered about the Sandy woman that they spoke of and what her involvement with them was, aside from being pregnant by him. I had so many questions that I knew he wouldn't give me the answers to, like how these two women even know each other, and why would they want each other to stay away from this Sandy person. Well, I know why she wanted him to stay away from her, it's the same reason I want both of these bitches out of our lives.

I allowed a couple weeks to pass before I went searching again for what I was looking for and yet again, I found it. I waited until he was high out of his mind and searched his phone. I found out that Sandy was a thorn in my husband's ass, and he couldn't stand her very existence. They argued through text messages constantly and she left him the meanest voicemails I had ever heard. It was surprising that they even had sex with each other. Kabrina on the other hand, he was obsessed with her. They talked all day, every day. Four-hour conversations during his workday, another hour on his lunch break, another hour conversation on his drive home, twenty and thirty minute calls while I knew he was here at home. Tears rolled down my face as I yearned to know what they were talking about. What could they possibly have to talk about throughout his day when he didn't even call to check on me that often? At

*most he calls once a day for a couple minutes and that's
after the boys are home from school, so we talk for a hot
second and then I pass the phone to the kids. I simply
couldn't believe it. My husband had a whole other life, and
I had no idea what was happening right under my nose.*

*I did my research and located Sandy in a rehab
center. Apparently, she had given birth prematurely and the
hospital made her get treatment for her drug and alcohol
abuse. He hadn't said shit about his daughter which meant
he either didn't know, or this was another one of his many
lies that I had exposed. I didn't know and I didn't care.
What I did care about was gathering information from this
woman. If they hated each other as much as it seemed
through their text messages, then maybe she would be
willing to spill what she knows.*

"Dr. Rebecca Blackwell for Sandra Smith."

*"Sign in Dr. Blackwell while I check the system." I
signed my name and twenty minutes later they took me to
the back. They assumed I was there on business and I
allowed them to. I need this information and I didn't care
what I had to do to get it.*

*Sandy walked into the room I was sitting in and I
couldn't believe my eyes or Brian. She was frail, her hair
was matted to her damn head, and she looked like she
smelled even though she didn't. I was immensely irritated
by her presence and disappointed that he would even stoop
to this level. Nothing about this crack whore was worth
cheating on me for. Nothing.*

*She laughed as she sat down. "You're Brian's wife,
right? How pathetic of you to be here."*

*Time she opened her mouth I understood why my
husband didn't like this woman but it still wasn't enough
for him to stay from between her legs. "How do you know
who I am?"*

*"I went to that white devil's office to tell him I was
pregnant with his child months ago, and there was a*

33

picture of you and y'all demonic offspring on his desk. What the fuck do you want with me Susan?"

"Are you in love with my husband?" There was no need to beat around any bushes.

"Are you smoking the same shit me and Brian smoke? Girl, please. I hate his white ass and the feeling is mutual."

"If you hate him so much, how do you two have a child together?"

She laughed again. "I was experimenting."

"Experimenting?"

"Yes Susan, experimenting! I wanted to suck on my best friend's pussy. That clear enough for you Boo?"

"What?"

"Oooo, you're in the dark. Did you even know I was pregnant with his child before I just told you?" She seemed amused.

"Yes. He told me. You're not the only one."

"Look at his white ass trying to be honest. Okay." She nodded. "I know I'm not. My best friend Kabrina is due any day now. They're in love and shit. Now she's talking about getting clean and all that other bullshit. I'm telling you right now. If she gets clean, he's leaving your honky ass for her. Bottomline. He worships the ground she walks on." A sadness came over her and that's when it all became clear to me. She was in love with Kabrina too.

"You love her, don't you?"

"Lady what the fuck do you want?"

"The whole truth and obviously I'm not going to get it from him."

"The truth is that your husband loves my best friend, he has for years. They have a long history together. The truth is that he doesn't give a fuck about the baby I gave birth too, but he's head over heels for the one she's carrying. The truth is that he's going to leave you for her. Like I said, they're in love."

34

"Can you give me more details?"

"Sure I can. It's going to cost you though."

"Cost me what?"

"I like to get high. The higher I am, the more I talk. This rehab shit is a joke. I'm just doing this so I can get my baby back from Kabrina. She has temporary custody of her because the hospital was on some bullshit after I had her."

I sat there for a moment taking in everything that she had said. Was Brian really going to throw away everything we worked for, to be with a crack whore from the ghetto? A chick who probably mirrored this tiny woman in front of me... "What's it going to be she-devil, tick tock?"

I stared at her with nothing but hate in my heart. These bitches were ruining my life. "I don't want your black ass baby anywhere near me or my husband. She's going to be a constant reminder that he fucked someone like you. I also don't want my husband around that other bitch either. If you help keep her away from him, I'll buy you all the drugs you want."

"And how do you want me to get in the way of true love Sue-Sue?" She smirked.

"Drugs. Keep her high and I'll keep him away and sober. Deal?" I extended my hand so we could shake on it.

"You have a deal but I'm not touching you. White people are evil, and your husband's touch was enough for a lifetime. I'm good on all that."

"Whatever. I'll be back tomorrow with what you want and when you get out of here don't forget our agreement."

"Just get me what the fuck I want, and I'll keep Kabrina high and happily single." No more words were spoken. I got up and walked out. I reached out to a friend from college and told him that I needed to knock the edge off, and he put me in contact with a man named Fernando that supplied him. What I didn't expect was for him to be as

gorgeous as he was. Fernando was a single father of two boys Ollie and Dominic who were just as gorgeous as their father. I don't know why I told Fernando about Brian and what I was going through but as soon as he asked me if I was single, I broke down crying and told him everything. My wounds were still open and raw, and I couldn't hold in my truth any longer. He wiped my tears and told me that I deserved better. I already knew that but to hear a man say it brought me comfort. This complete stranger held me while I cleansed my soul and then offered to supply me with exactly what I needed, when I needed it. I had to keep Kabrina away from my husband and I was willing to do anything, to do so. Thanks to Fernando, I would be able to do just that.

PRESENT

"Ahhhh." I screamed out as beads of sweat formed above my eyebrow.

"Relax Rebecca. I have to change your dressing." Smitty, Fernando's right hand man said to me as I continued to wince in pain. I couldn't help it. The pain that was shooting through me was the most pain I've felt since childbirth. "They got you pretty good, but you're fine cry baby." He passed me two pills and a cup of water. "Take these. They'll help with the pain."

"You sure about that? Nothing has worked so far."

"Just take the pills." I looked behind me and Fernando and Dominic were sitting with stoic expressions on their faces leaving me unable to read the situation. It had been a full day since everything went down and I hadn't seen either of them until now.

"Thanks, Smitty," I said after taking the pills. He nodded and walked out.

"Explain why you left my son in a house full of enemies? Explain why you left my son and drove yourself to safety not giving a fuck whether he lived or died in that house. Explain to me why you--"

"What the hell do you mean Fernando?" I yelled, cutting his bullshit rant off. "Your fuckin' nephew and my stepdaughter tried to kill me! Twice! Look at my knees! Look at the damn holes in me! I had mere seconds to make it out of there alive or I wouldn't be here to have this conversation. I called you as soon as I pulled off to send more help. That's all I could do."

"You froze like I said you would which is why the fuck you shouldn't have been there in the first fuckin' place!" His voice roared throughout the room and he hopped up. We'd argued for three days about whether I could pull the trigger on my family or not and I swore I could. "I knew you wouldn't do it and you didn't, and you could have cost my son his fuckin' life! The only son that I have left!" His voice boomed again causing me to jump. I didn't know what he wanted from me, when they were trying to fucking kill me. That last bullet before Messiah stopped Jax from shooting, hit me in the side and I had to crawl through the shattered glass from the windows, just to get to the front of the van where I could barely even pull off from the pain I was enduring.

He stared at me with fire burning in his eyes. "The next time I tell your ass you can't do something you'd better fuckin' listen and listen both closely and carefully. You're way too close to this emotionally and I told you that before we even took Nashon out. I saw you crying when you saw how hurt Jaxsyn was and what did I tell you, Rebecca?" He came closer and I looked in the opposite direction. "What did I tell you?" He yelled and tears started rolling down my face.

"That I was too close, and you would handle everything." I answered barely above a whisper.

"That *I* would handle things." He grabbed my face tight, making me look at him.

"Pop." Dominic spoke up before things went left and I was grateful. "I walked out of the bitch untouched, and we still have collateral. Let's go map this shit out and end these muthafuckas for good." He stood and walked over to us because Fernando hadn't budged, and I was in a full-blown emotional breakdown as he stared a hole into me. This was a side of him that scared me to death. This was the side that I used to find attractive because it was never directed towards me, but everything changed when he found out that Jaxsyn was dating his nephew. I wish I had never said anything, but how was I supposed to know they had history. "Come on." Dominic tapped his back and after an awkward moment of him still staring at me he tossed my head back like I was trash.

"Get out."

"What?"

"I'm not repeating myself. Smitty will make sure all your shit is delivered to wherever your feet land. I'll call you when I calm down because right now, I want to blow your fuckin' head off, and if you stay in my presence, that's exactly what the fuck is going to happen."

"Fernando what was I supposed to do? Huh? They were shooting at me! Sandy's brains were all over me! Jaxsyn fired five shots back-to-back before Messiah stopped her because of my grand--" I stopped myself and he smirked, but it was dark and concealing his anger.

"Your *granddaughter*?" He nodded his head. "Make sure she's out of here within the hour. I'll meet you in the office after that. I need a scotch." He walked away and I broke down.

"Dominic. I'm sorry. I never meant to leave you Baby, but I knew we had men there and I was just trying to--"

"Save yourself." He cut me off as he looked back at me over his shoulder. "You were thinking about you and only you. You took off in the fuckin' truck that I drove us there in, so if Uncle Jose hadn't been with us and the other guys hadn't been close, I would have been dead. You gambled with my life. I may not want him to put his hands on you, but you're done in my book."

"Dominic." I stepped closer to him and he allowed me to. "Please don't do this." I ran my hand down his chest and I could see the bulge in his pants growing but before I could make another move, he slapped my hand down.

"I'm Gato to you from now on. He'll fuck with you once he calms down because he loves you, but from this day forward, you ain't shit to me but a bitch that I shared a few good memories with." He walked out and I wailed. Dominic and Ollie have been like sons to me, but Dominic and I shared so much more than what the naked eye could see. My heart was shattered by his words and actions, probably more than Fernando's.

Our intentions were to draw Messiah out that night, but we weren't there to kill anyone. We were going to kidnap his grandmother and force his ass to come clean about his father's operation. This was supposed to be a win-win situation. Kabrina would be killed after being a thorn in my side for over twenty years. Messiah would tell Fernando how to take down his father Mauricio's empire, and we would fake my death in the process so I could finally be with Fernando the way we've both been longing for. My children are all grown now, and my work is done. Once Fernando takes what he wants from his little brother he's moving us to Colombia, but now I don't know where we stand, and Dominic hates me. Messiah needed to pay for the constant pain that he keeps causing me.

"You ready?" Smitty came walking into the room I was in.

"No. I'm shot Smitty."

39

"He doesn't care Becca. He wants you gone, *now*."

"Where am I supposed to go? Everyone knows I betrayed my family!"

"That's not our problem." Dominic walked back into the room rolling a suitcase. "We'll send the rest to wherever you decide to go."

"Son."

"Don't you dare do that!" He yelled. "I know for a fact you would have never left Dawson and Jagger for dead so don't you ever in your fuckin' life refer to me as your son again. Those days been over for a long time anyway, so don't play with me. Get the fuck off of our property until he wants to look at you again." He looked at Smitty. "Now," he said as he walked away and Smitty came over to me and grabbed me by the arm, forcefully pulling me off of the bed. I screamed and cried but it was nothing I could do. Fernando is the head of a cartel, what he says goes and Dominic is next in line, so his word holds just as much weight.

"Please, Smitty. Pleeeeease." I begged and he ignored me until I was in the front seat of his car gasping for air from crying so hard.

"Where to?"

"I. Don't. Knooow." I panted, trying to regain my composure.

"Where Rebecca?"

"A hotel." I stared out of the window at Fernando's estate. I couldn't believe he was doing this to me after everything we had been to each other. He knew better than anyone that I had no one. Literally. Jaxsyn probably already told her father everything, but then again, there was a possibility that she didn't. She damn sure hadn't told us about the kids being kidnapped which was a part of the original plan, but we had to readjust when they decided to handle it privately. If she hadn't told Brian anything, that would buy me a little time to get myself together and figure out my next move. There was also the possibility that Lyss would say something, but I knew she would be so messed up after seeing what happened to Sandy that her ass would probably dash back to her school to wrap her mind around what she witnessed. Either way, they would both give me the much-needed time before Brian found out.

I had to try reaching out just in case it was all playing out in real life how it was playing out in my mind. I pulled my phone out of my purse and powered it on. There were thirteen voicemails waiting on me, but my first call was to Brian before listening to any of them.

"Hello." He answered with his regular tone of voice which gave me hope. Playing it cool, I cleared my throat.

"Hey baby." I perked up to sound like I normally would.

"You're as good as dead Rebecca. If you know me like you claim you do, then you already knew that." His voice was still calm, but harsh, a deadly combination for him. He hung up and a pain shot through my heart. My fingers went straight to the location settings on my phone and turned it off. I couldn't take any chances of him finding me or giving out my location. There were so many people coming after me all because I was trying to help the man I love. The same man that had just turned his back on me, and kicked me out of his home, as I was losing my whole family for the second time in my life…

Guess karma wasn't handing out grace periods.

Alyssa Blackwell

I rocked back and forth while I waited to find out what was happening with Messiah. Images of who I now know was Sandy, were etched into my memories and the tears wouldn't stop falling. All I kept seeing over and over was the bullet from Sih's smoking gun enter her head while blood and matter sprayed everywhere. The way her body jerked, and head exploded on one side was on repeat and being in this creepy ass basement alone didn't help.

Over the last couple years, I've grown to love Messiah just as much as I love Dawson and Jagger. He was my brother, and I didn't see him any other way. Considering he made my sister put her anger on hold, to trust me, showed that he loved me too. Jax still didn't want me anywhere near them, but I wanted to know if my brother was okay just like she did.

We had been at this person Doc's house for hours upon hours and she refused to tell me anything that was going on with Sih, or even come back downstairs to check on me. She told me to wait in the basement and never returned. I asked to hold my niece and she damn near screamed *no* at me. My feelings were crushed. Never in a million years would I bring harm to her, the kids, or Sih, but she was treating me like the enemy. Treating me like she hadn't been my best friend since birth and knew me better than anyone. I couldn't say I blamed her entirely, considering the circumstances, but me understanding her didn't stop my heart from shattering.

When I saw my mother holding a gun, I was instantly taken aback, but to see that gun pointed at my sister and Sih completely threw me off. Rebecca Ann Blackwell was many things, but a murderer... kidnapper...

snake? None of that made sense to me. It just didn't. She's helped my daddy with Jax since she was a baby. She's literally watched her grow up and never once did she treat Jax differently than the rest of us when Jax came over. This was hard for me to wrap my mind around, but I didn't have any choice. I saw her with my own two eyes and now I can't un-see it or ignore it. I just needed to know why.

I wiped my tear-soaked face and stood to leave. It was obvious Jax wasn't about to allow me to comfort her, hold my niece, or check on Messiah, so I really had no reason to be here at all. I ordered an Uber and made my way upstairs. The home we were in was beautiful and had such a homey feel. It was warm and inviting.

"Being sneaky like your mother?" I had one hand on the doorknob to exit the home but stopped at the sound of Jaxsyn's voice. I turned around and she was sitting on the couch in the living room rocking Nevaeh to sleep. I could see the pain in her eyes, and I wanted nothing more than to hug her and tell her everything would work out for the best, but along with that pain and sadness that her eyes held was anger, and lots of it.

"No Jax. You left me in the basement, so I ordered an Uber to leave."

"So you can go report back to your mother about where we are? You trying to give her and her goons a heads up so they can come finish the job?" She chuckled evilly to herself and it cut deep.

"Come on Jax, that's not fair. That's not fair at all." I instantly started crying again. I was an emotional wreck. "Stop acting like you don't know me, I would nev--"

"I thought I fuckin' knew her too!" She yelled and then looked down. My niece was still knocked out sleeping in her arms and she kissed her head. "Make sure when you tell that bitch where we are that you tell her she better bring a fuckin' army because we ain't takin' no more shorts this way. You tell that snake ass bitch put her game face on because I'm out for nothing but blood." Her tone was cold and laced with hate. I didn't know if that hate was directed at me or the whole situation, but it broke me down anyway.

"I would never in my life hurt you or my nieces and nephew. Never in my life…" I gasped, "would I hurt Sih or anyone else I love. I don't know why she did this, how she did this, or who she did this with, but it wasn't me and it hurts to the core of my existence that you would think that I would ever condone or participate in something so vile. You've been my best friend and idol my whole life Jax."

She stared at me and now I was thinking that maybe the anger her eyes held, coupled with disgust, was directed straight at me. It became extremely uncomfortable, and right as I was about to reach for the door handle again, she spoke,

"Fuck you, your core, your existence, your mother, and every other raggedy bitch that may have had a hand in this. My fuckin' son is still missing, and I'll burn every square inch of this fuckin' city down to the ground until I have him back with me, his father and his sisters. When you see that bitch, just deliver the message, and then wrap your mind around being a motherless child like I'm doing since she probably killed Kabrina." She got up and walked out. I couldn't believe this was happening and the pain in my chest was intense.

****

"Mmmm." I moaned out and gripped the sheets. The room was pitch black, but the smell of Gucci Guilty Black invaded my nostrils. "Sssss yes! Just like that." I rolled my hips as waves of euphoria rushed over me. I had so much going on and this moment of pleasure to ease some of the stress I was feeling, was needed like my next breath. My legs quivered as my kitty contracted and showered Kevin with a flow of my juices that even surprised me. "Ughhhh." I groaned when he didn't stop, allowing another orgasm to tear into my soul. This was everything I needed.

"I could watch you cum everyday all day, beautiful." I could see him even through the darkness of our room and we both smiled. My smile was cut short as he slid inside of me taking my breath away. "Kevvvv," I purred.

"Yes baby?" He went deeper and I dug my nails into his back. He's told me about doing that shit a million times, but he knows when he goes that deep, I can't take it. "What I tell you?" He gently bit my neck as he repositioned me to the edge of the bed and stood on the side.

"I'm sor--" My voice got caught in my throat as he stuffed me with every inch he had to offer.

"I told you about the scratches, right?" He kept digging like he had a map, and it was gold waiting to be found. I started screaming his name and he plowed me mercilessly. His sweat was dripping on me, my legs were shaking, and he was talking mad shit. "Fuck!" He pulled out and came on my stomach. "You have to stop Lyss. I mean that shit. Not because she knows about us mean I'm trying to throw it in her face."

"I'm sorry Kevin but honestly it's not on purpose. Stop going so deep and I'll stop reacting like that."

He kissed me and shook his head no, as he reached over and turned the lamp on. "I have to go."

"Yeah... I know." I rolled my eyes and he sighed.

"Don't start. Please. You called me at four in the morning Lyss, and I came to you. What more do you want from me?"

"Well for starters, I want you to ask me why I called you this late and not just treat me like a fuckin' whore. Then since we're on the subject of what I want from you, let's address the baby I'm carrying Kevin." Again, he sighed. I never expected any of this to happen between us. I

45

never planned on having sex with a married man and definitely not one that I was introduced to by a classmate who happens to be his daughter. Granted, we weren't friends, but he's definitely old enough to be my father and this was wrong on many levels. I couldn't even pinpoint when I fell in love with him, but I did, and when he finally admitted to feeling the same way, we became careless. So careless that his wife Heather found out and dangled telling his kids the truth over his head if he didn't stop seeing me. Unfortunately, he couldn't, and her words didn't hold the weight she assumed they would. Now I'm pregnant and she's known about us for about six months now. She calls my phone constantly and threatens me. This is going to turn both of our lives upside down. Ignoring it won't change a damn thing which is what he's been trying to do since I told him.

"I apologize baby. Why did you call me?" He sat on the side of the bed and I stared at him for a moment and then told him as much as I could about the night I stumbled upon. All I wanted to do was pick up some things from granny Knight to surprise my sister with, and I messed around and got caught up in drama that I was still having trouble grasping. "Damn. That's straight out of a movie."

"It is. I was so scared, and then all that was washed away by the pain and anger in my sister's eyes. She hates me for something that I didn't even know about." I started crying for the millionth time and he brought me into his arms. His touch and his familiar scent made me cry harder for some reason. I needed him and although he wasn't home when I got here, he got out of his bed with his wife and came to me. This is how I got caught up. I loved him from the depths of my soul, and he gave me peace in the midst of all my storms.

"You have to calm down Alyssa. You're going to stress the baby out." My head popped up and I looked at him. He smirked and wiped my face. I'm two months pregnant, and it was him that suggested I take a test. He's a doctor so I didn't even hesitate to take one and it came back positive. He couldn't even utter the word baby let alone acknowledge the test was positive. The only thing I could appreciate is the fact that not one time did he ask me to get an abortion or ask what I was going to do.

"What?" I needed to hear him say it again. He thumbed the fresh tears away and kissed my lips.

"Calm down before you cause my baby, *our* baby, unnecessary stress. Your sister is pissed right now, and she should be. Her children were missing and hell, one of them still is. That's a lot to go through. I imagine it would be even harder if the person you've called mother was the one to do it, right?" I nodded. "Exactly. Give her time, baby. If you're struggling to wrap your mind around it, you know she can't even begin to fathom the whirlwind she's been thrown into. Don't take her words to heart, just show her that you're still her baby sister that idolizes her every move."

"I love you." I hugged him and he held me tightly.

"I love you too, baby." We stayed entwined in each other's arms for a few more moments and I knew when he started pulling away, he had to go.

"Am I seeing you later?"

"Yeah. I did some light grocery shopping earlier. I told Heather I'll be working a double, so I'll be home tonight. Have that pussy out and ready for me."

"Yes sir." I giggled and kissed him goodbye. He bought us a condo a few months back and when he's not home with his family, he's home with me. I didn't know how this was going to work but I just knew that as long as I had even a sliver of his love and attention, I would be quite alright.

Messiah

My eyes popped open from the intense pain in my chest. I was about to wild the fuck out because it felt like I was being weighed down but thank God I looked before I reacted, it was Jax and Nevaeh. Jax was in my arms and baby girl was on the left side of my chest, opposite of where the pain was coming from. I stared at her for what seemed like forever. Our reunion was bittersweet because her brother was still missing but my heart swelled in my chest and I couldn't even hold back the tears when I first laid eyes on her. Our world was rocked as we watched that hoe ass nigga Dominic drop her and Junior on the video that we had to watch over and over. Each time it ripped at our hearts and broke us down a little further but having her lying on my chest was indescribable.

I rubbed their heads until the sun started shining through the window and Jax started to stir. I didn't know where the fuck we were, but I knew if she was peacefully sleeping in my arms, she felt safe.

"Good morning, Tink," I said and she damn near jumped out of her skin.

"Messiah! Baby!" Her kisses rained down on me and I couldn't do shit but smile. The love I have for this woman was deep and on a level that I didn't even know existed. I could tell her I love her a million times a day and she still wouldn't have a clue as to how deep my love truly runs for her. "I was so scared. I thought--"

"Nah. Come here." I pulled her up some and returned the kisses she had just given me. She smirked when I parted her lips with my tongue. As we kissed, I felt her relaxing into my embrace. I wiped the single tear that fell from her eye and made her open her eyes to look at me.

48

"I told you I was coming back, and I meant it." I pecked her lips. "Just like I told you we're going to find our son and we will."

"Promise me Messiah. I'm on the fuckin' edge Bae and I'm trying so hard to keep my shit together."

"I know you are and it's okay to be on the edge. Shit, I'm on that bitch with you and shit just got deeper, but ain't no given up Jax. Ain't no jumpin' off baby. We in this shit together and Junior is coming home Tink, I promise." I could see the pain in her eyes, and I hoped, wished, and prayed that she didn't checkout on me again. Seeing her hurting so deeply fucked with me every day and I couldn't go through that again and neither could she.

"I miss him so much." She broke down in my arms and tugged at a nigga's heart in a major way. I couldn't even hold my own tears back. I swear I was trying to be strong for both of us, but knowing that my son was in the possession of a nigga that had his people to fire a rocket launcher into a house that he was in himself, is fuckin' with me. That's a different level of crazy…

My son was supposed to be home in his mother's arms, playing with daddy, or chasing behind his sisters. My fuckin' blood was boiling and running cold all at the same time just thinking about what this lunatic may have done to my baby boy. This whole situation needed to be taken care of immediately. Repeatedly comforting Jaxsyn without giving her results was a dub. Constantly asking her to trust me bringing our son home without at least giving her something to believe in, was heavily weighing on my mental and a fuckin' dub too. My word wasn't shit at this point. Nothing was getting better, and the reality of our situation was that shit was actually getting deeper by the day.

"Me too, baby." I kissed her head and gave her a few more minutes before I asked what happened. All I remember is one of my cousins yelling *run* and another saying *rocket launcher* while Dominic or Gato, whatever the fuck they call him, laughed hysterically in the chair he was tied to. We all ran for the front door as the rocket launcher came busting through the window causing an explosion. Everything after that, I can't remember.

"I don't know baby. One minute I'm sitting in the car talking to my father and then the next minute, an explosion in the house is shaking the car like--" She sighed. "I just… I didn't think baby. I couldn't… I hopped out with Nevaeh on my hip and Alyssa on my ass. We were calling your name and found Solo, Glen, and Jason standing over you."

"What!"

"Exactly, so I'm holding them at gunpoint telling them to get the fuck away from you, when Solo tells me that Gizmo told them about the meet up. He had them to fall back. Giz said you wasn't thinking clear or some shit. Anyway, I had the gun on they asses ready to pull the trigger when a car came barreling through the alley and Solo snatched me up and had Glen and Jason grab you as we ran to the car. You had metal from the explosion in your chest and were unconscious. Solo was yelling for your cousins that was in Grandma Knight's front yard to duck, and then all hell broke loose. Gunshots coming from every direction, police sirens could be heard in the distance, Nevaeh was crying, Alyssa was screaming, and Solo was yelling at me to drive off. It got crazy as hell."

"Damn, baby." I kissed her head repeatedly. She didn't deserve this bullshit. When we first met, all she wanted was peace and happiness. My promise was to give her that. Yet she had just lived through a scene from Grand Theft Auto. My manhood was taking hit after hit, but my personal feelings had to take a backseat. "You know where my phone is? I need to check on everybody." She peeled herself out of my arms, grabbed her purse, and passed it to me. I repositioned baby girl on my chest and powered it on. Time that bitch lit up I hit send on Giz number.

"Nigga." He took a deep breath. "Cuz, you can't be pulling disappearing acts, it's too much shit going on."

"Aye, it wasn't on purpose. They blew the house up and Jax said some shit hit me in the chest."

"I know they did and then yo' ass disappeared. Where you at? I got some information and you ain't about to like shit I got to say."

"I don't even know. Hol' up." I turned to Jax. "Baby, where we at?"

"Doc's house."

"Who?"

She stared at me.

"Doc."

"Is it yo people, because I don't know a nigga named Doc?" I sat up more and looked at her and her facial expression started changing.

"Solo said--" She stopped and looked around nervously. "Solo said take him to Doc so I just--"

"Giz, I'm about to send you my location cuz."

"Bet."

"Aye," I said before he hung up. "Did you tell Solo where we would be last night?"

"Yeah man. I looked into that nigga while you were locked up. My gut told me he was good people's, but you were so fucked up behind Nash that you shut everybody down. He ain't have shit to do with shit and we about to get deeper into what actually happened but yeah, I had that nigga to watch the house. I had a feeling they would hit granny's house and not Jax parents' house."

"Nigga that's because her stepmom was in on it."

"Oh, I know. I'm telling you now, shit deeper than that. I'm on my way." He hung up and I shook my head then sent my location.

"What? What he say?"

"He did tell Solo, but I guess he got some information that's about to make this shit even deeper."

"Can we even handle deeper right now?" She looked more annoyed than sad, and I understood completely.

"Good morning."

"Maaaan, nigga she kept calling you Doc and that shit threw me off. I didn't know where the fuck she had me. Baby his name is Daulph."

"She was a nervous wreck when she got here so I wasn't about to correct her." We slapped hands and Jax shook her head.

"You had me nervous like I had us somewhere we weren't supposed to be."

"Shit, you had me nervous too because I don't know a nigga name Doc." All three of us laughed and then he told me that he had to give me nineteen stitches in my chest to close the wounds the metal shavings caused. He also said I had a concussion and he'd checked out Nevaeh. We were both good. He passed me a couple Motrin 800's and told me to get my ass up. We'd been knowing Daulph since he was in college becoming a doctor. I've brought a shit ton of my guys to him wounded but I never had to see him for myself. Until now.

"Solo just left. I thought y'all were still sleep. He said he'll hit you later."

"Bet. My cousin Gizmo is on his way here, let security know."

"I got you." He walked out and I sat up while Jax took Nevaeh out of my arms. My chest was sore as hell, but I had shit to do, and no amount of pain was going to stop that. I popped the Motrin and started preparing my mind for whatever Giz was about to come with.

****

Daulph's wife Octavia cooked breakfast and we all sat down and ate. I tried my best to act like I gave a fuck about the conversation that was taking place, but I had too much shit running through my head. I still hadn't heard back from Fresh about Kabrina, so I texted him while she was on my mind. I had been thinking about my son and this information that was coming my way so much that I almost forgot that shit Sandy said about Kabrina. I really hoped that bitch was lying or didn't hear that nigga Gato correctly. Jax honestly couldn't take much more. One person can only take so much and my Tink had surpassed her limit.

"Hello." I got up and walked away from the table.

"Somebody snatched her up out of there. The backdoor was off the hinges, it was broken glass and furniture everywhere, and drops of blood went from her living room all the way out of the backdoor."

"Fuck."

"Not enough blood for her to be dead though. Well, it didn't happen in the house if she is."

"Alright."

"I'll hit you later. I'm about to take granny something to eat real quick. She made us get her a room at a five-star hotel. She took one look at the shack in the woods and told us we had her fucked up." We both laughed and ended the call. Eugena Knight is always going to do whatever the fuck she wants to do and can't nobody stop her lil feisty ass.

I heard the doorbell and went back to the kitchen to wait for my cousin. A nigga was anxious as fuck. I needed to know whatever Giz knew, and he couldn't come through that door quick enough. I took my seat next to Jax and she searched my face to see if my mood had changed and then kissed me.

"Messiah. You're a hard man to get in contact with these days." Lace walked in and I didn't feel like dealing

53

with this shit right now. She and I do business together but that wasn't always the case. We used to fuck with each other heavy before Mariah and every time Mariah and I were on our typical bullshit. It started out on some business shit I had going with her brother. When he got killed over a bitch he was kickin' it with, she took over and started fuckin' shit up. She came to me for guidance and ended up swallowing my dick that same night. That went on for eight months before I officially made Mariah my girl. They hated each other before I told her to chill the fuck out and respect my situation. I hadn't even hit yet, and she was trippin'. That first time me and Mariah broke up Lace wasted no time hopping on this dick and she's been hooked ever since. That's why I sent her ass down south when I got with Jax.

"I'm always where I need to be. What you doin' here, you holla at Solo?"

"I did, which is how I know where you are. Now I need to holla at you," she said seductively while eye fuckin' me.

"Excuse us." Octavia stood up with a raised eyebrow and Daulph followed her lead without looking our way. I wish they hadn't done that because it made this shit seem like more than what it was. I haven't fucked with Lace since before I even met Jax and sent her ass packing when shit got serious with us. She was old news and we both knew it, regardless of the tone she was standing in front of me using.

"What business do y'all have together?" Jax looked at me and Nevaeh reached for me. As soon as my daughter was in my arms she started staring up at Lace and I wanted to laugh. So, this is going to be my life with a house full of women.

"She's in charge of distro in the south, baby. That's it."

"Mm." Jax turned her attention back to Lace, "You found him, say what you have to say so you can go." Lace turned her lip up and was about to say something smart, but I intervened.

"What you want Lace?"

"We never spoke in front of Mariah so I would prefer--"

"Neither one of us gives a fuck about your preferences. Speak now or forever hold your peace *Lace*." Jax was in rare form but I knew from that ass whippin' she gave Mariah at the picnic that this shit could go left real quick. Lace wasn't going to go down as easily as Mariah and these two would damn sure tear Daulph's whole fuckin' house up over nothing. Lace wasn't shit to me but a worker, and Jax knows ain't nobody fuckin' with her spot.

"What up, cuz." Giz walked in at the perfect time.

"Sissy." Nevaeh wiggled to get out of my arms and went running towards Z and Jeniah. They hugged each other and we all smiled. I squeezed Jax's hand. This moment was bittersweet, I knew her mind probably went straight to Junior missing out on the love fest.

"Lace, can you get up with Solo again about whatever it is. I have a lot of shit going on right now. He's capable of dealing with whatever it is, like he always does."

"So he's capable of handling ten million in pills and cash gone from your warehouse in Georgia? He's able to handle last night's shipment going missing too, which is another twenty million in medical supplies and the injectable medications? He got that covered *Boss*?" She folded her arms as I felt my blood boiling and running cold again. I felt dizzy like a nigga was about to pass out. Shit was coming from every direction. Gato was begging for the attention I was about to give his ass.

"When the fuck did that happen and why the fuck didn't you lead with that?"

"She was too busy trying to fuck you." Jax rolled her eyes.

"*Actually* sweetheart, been there, done that." Lace rolled her neck and eyes. "I tried calling you several times the other day and last night when it happened. I was also trying to tell you just now, but I didn't know we could talk in front of… company."

"Hoe, I'm his fiancée, not company, and you let some more slick shit leave that cum receptacle on your face and I'm going to dog walk yo' ass all through these people's house. I'm not Mariah hoe, play with me if you want to and you're going to fuck around and be a headline."

"Na, what's going on?" Z walked up ready to wreck some shit with her sister and I stood. This shit wasn't about to go down. We had other shit that needed our attention, and this wasn't even close to making the list.

"Nothing. Lace, watch how the fuck you address my woman and keep that old shit in the past. I'm about to have my cousin Fresh meet up with you so he can handle this shit. Go to the main warehouse and he'll be there shortly." I shot Fresh a text and told him after he finished with granny to go get up with Lace. She looked pissed, but I didn't give a fuck and stared her ass down until she turned around and quietly walked out. I could feel Jax burning a hole through my ass, so I didn't even look her way. Like I said, at this point, she's well aware that I don't want none of these random hoes so instead of entertaining her shit, I addressed Gizmo, "tell me everything you know." I had been anxiously waiting for this nigga all morning and that petty ass drama wasn't about to delay me from hearing what he had to say another moment.

I walked into the living room and he followed with Jax and Z right behind him. "Tell your pops to come in here too." He looked at them and Jax rolled her eyes before Z turned back around to go get him.

"Syd, Dawson, and Jagger are about to eat breakfast so they can just play in here while we talk." Zionna was holding Jeniah and Nevaeh's hands when she came back with Brian. We simply nodded with a smile as we watched our girls happily play without a care in the world.

"Alright, so check this out." He leaned forward with his elbows on his knees. "I told you that you and the nigga Gato crossed paths too many times, but the shit is way deeper than that. His father is your father's big brother. The nigga is your first cousin."

"What?" I sat back confused.

"A lot of coincidences lead us to this very moment which is crazy as hell but hear me out." He turned to Brian. "Your bitch been cheating on you for years bro, and with the same guy. Ol' boy's name is Fernando Vargas. Dude is the head of the Vargas Cartel and one dangerous muthafucka. He's the one that supplied Rebecca with the drugs that got Sandy on board to keep you and Kabrina apart."

"Keep y'all apart?" Jax said as she looked at Brian for the first time since he walked in.

"Wow..." You could see the pain and confusion written all over Brian's face, but the redness of his ears showed he was also mad as hell. "Kabrina and I fell in love as kids. She was my whole world, and we were destined to be together. No one could tell us any different." He leaned forward and reached into his back pocket pulling his wallet out. He dug in it and took out a picture of them from when they were kids, hugged up and smiling from ear to ear. Jax's eyes filled with tears and I squeezed her hand. "We were inseparable until her parents let us know that she was going to Clark Atlanta with her cousins, and it wasn't up for debate. We had plans but her mother wanted her far away from me. I was hanging around my cousins who were heavily into that street life while Kabrina was a straight A student, and her parent's golden child. They wanted to put some space between us and nothing we said mattered a damn. Distance did to us, the same shit it does to everyone else; caused loneliness, doubt, jealousy, and unfaithfulness.

"Within a year we barely talked and when we did, it always ended in a shouting match that we would later have to apologize for. After a while I said fuck it. I was done arguing with her ass about everything, so I stopped calling and answering. One night she called me back-to-back, and I instantly knew something was wrong. It was four a.m., and she had a seven-a.m. class the next day. She's crying hysterically and tell me that she was raped at some party she went to with her new friends. It didn't happen on campus or by someone that went to the school so the school couldn't do shit. Then the male officers that responded, acted as if Kabrina asked for it because of the little shorts she was wearing. That shit fucked her head up and less than six months later she flunked out. She met Sandy when she got back to Detroit and I could instantly tell that she was a bad influence.

"Kabrina started doing more drugs than we previously dabbled in and she drank like a fish. Every time I called to check on her, she was high, drunk, or both. By the time I graduated and came back home she was knee deep in the streets with Sandy, and everything I had heard from my cousins was true. I still tried to rock with her anyway, but she was different, too different. My feelings for her hadn't changed, but she needed help and more attention than I could give her at the time. I knew where her pain came from and I wanted to help her heal but she wasn't trying to hear me.

"Unfortunately, my one-night stand with Rebecca before leaving school changed my life. Rebecca found out she was pregnant and before she told me, she told her family. They found out I had black people in my family and that I had never been with a white woman before Rebecca and told her to get an abortion and leave me alone. She refused the abortion and they disowned her. The last thing they wanted was a mixed child running around their family, so I had to step up not only for the kid she was carrying, but for her too. She had nowhere to go and no one to turn to. Kabrina was crushed. No matter what happened between us, I felt like we both believed we would still end up together and now here I was telling her that I got another girl pregnant, and we were moving in together.

"When you love someone as much as I love her, when that person is in pain, you hurt with them, and I instantly tried to make shit right with her. We started messing around again and that went on for quite a while but when Rebecca turned up pregnant again, Kabrina was done with my ass. Completely. We didn't see each other or even talk to each other for about three years, when my cousin invited me to her thirtieth birthday party.

"Kabrina attended and like a moth to a flame, we were all over each other. We missed each other so much and I knew then that Kabrina was never going to leave my heart. We started kicking it again and Sandy, who was still around, hated it. She felt like I was taking Kabrina away from her and I was. Kabrina shouldn't have been hanging with her anyway. Sandy was older and into a bunch of bullshit that Bri had never even been exposed to. The influence that Sandy had over Kabrina was ruining her, and I knew Kabrina was better than the shit she was doing.

"One-night Sandy came over and we're all getting high. She started talking Kabrina into a threesome that I wasn't feeling at all. Sandy's persistence was hard to ignore, so after a while, neither of us fought her."

"Damn straight." Giz smiled and we all shook our heads at this fool.

"It turned out to be the worst decision of my life. Sandy got pregnant and threw that shit in Kabrina's face. She said some slick shit like *'damn, everybody havin' Brian's baby but you'* and laughed at Bri. I watched

59

Kabrina's heart break all over again, and she started spiraling out of control. I told Rebecca about Sandy and she was pissed, but before we could even fully bounce back from that, Kabrina came to me and told me she was pregnant too.

"We had made up and was catching up on time missed. We were high and careless one too many times and next thing I know, Kabrina is crying hysterically and telling me that she was pregnant. I wasn't even mad. I was actually excited, and Rebecca picked up on it when I finally sat her down and told her. She called me out on it but no matter what my mouth said, I couldn't hide how I felt, so eventually, I kept it real with her." He shrugged his shoulders as we all sat there stunned by how this shit really played out between all of them. I don't even think Jax, or Z knew the real story. By the expressions on their faces, it damn sure didn't seem like they knew. "I wanted my family, so I told Rebecca what she wanted to hear, the truth. She begged me to go to rehab. She felt like drugs had warped my brain and that was the reason I was making the decisions that I was making. I knew Bec wouldn't lay off so I begged Kabrina to do it with me. She was pregnant and battling with her inner demons. She didn't want to hurt our baby but the pain she felt inside kept her going back to the drugs.

"Eventually, her past and Sandy's hold on her, outweighed mine. Kabrina progressively got worse. I had no idea that it was all a plot against her. Against our love." His voice cracked. "When Jax went to college I knew her heart was broken. Jax never shied away from wanting to escape so I went over to Kabrina's house and found her crying with a gallon of Five O'clock vodka. She told me that she drove her baby to hate her and that she was tired of living. She laid in my arms for hours crying over Jax and all the fucked-up decisions that she'd made. Her heart was broken, and she had hit her rock bottom. The next day, I sent her to rehab. She relapsed and I sent her ass right back. When she finished a hundred and twenty days out here, I sent her to California for another nine months in a sober living facility. She end up staying a year and I visited her every family day or visitation day. I encouraged her, motivated her, prayed for her, and loved her through her process. When she came back, she was my old Kabrina. The light in her eyes that I've always loved had returned and I was beyond proud of her." He looked up at Jax. "We umm, we've... been together ever since."

"Excuse me?" Jax eyebrows caved inward.

"Daddy." Sydnee, who we hadn't even noticed, covered her face.

"Damn..." I sat back and shook my head.

"We're in love, and Rebecca has always known. I'm not saying cheating on Rebecca was right, I'm not saying that at all, but the heart wants what it wants, and my heart wouldn't let Kabrina go, so I stopped trying to fight it and followed it instead."

"Well, you weren't the only one so don't kick yourself too much. Rebecca ain't no Mother Theresa. Her relationship with Fernando afforded her the opportunity to make a deal with Sandy. Drugs on demand to make sure she kept Kabrina high and away from you and to also keep Zionna away too. One outside child was one too many for Rebecca, and she played on you and Sandy hating each other.

Fast forward, Jax randomly meets the nephew that Fernando is convinced is running his brother Mauricio's empire. Come to find out, Mauricio didn't even know about you and Nash. Fernando had both of his sons and his other nephew gunning for y'all, not knowing y'all didn't even know his brother. I got in touch with Mauricio and the nigga on his way out here. He didn't take it too well that he had sons that he didn't know about and he took it even harder when I told him about Nash. He instantly said he would be here soon and hung up. That was after midnight last night and he called me right before I got here to tell me he'd just arrived. I think we should holla at him."

"Damn man." I was trying to take in everything he said but that shit was overwhelming. I've been hating my father my whole life. Me and Nash had to fight and claw our way out of poverty, and we hated this nigga for leaving us. Finding out he never even knew about us caused a weird ass feeling. I still wanted to hate him. At the same time, my cousin called this dude and he dropped everything to be here. This was some more shit to add to the million things I already had resting on my shoulders.

Zionna

Jax paced from one side of the room, to the other. She was pissed about her parents creeping around behind everyone's backs, but after the story settled into my mental, I thought it was rather cute. Brian shouldn't have been cheating on Rebecca and that's probably what pushed her into making these stupid ass moves. He was definitely wrong for that, but like he said, the heart wants what the heart wants. Obviously, time, distance, marriage, and drugs weren't enough to stop Brian and Kabrina from loving each other. That shit was cute as hell to me in a twisted adulterous way.

"Hey." Messiah swaggered into the kitchen. Jax walked into his embrace and he whispered something into her ear before kissing her and they turned towards me. "We need to talk to you."

"Okay." They both looked nervous, so I was instantly on high alert as to what they were about to say. Jax was literally pacing the floor which I now see was for this conversation and not her parents at all. This had to be serious.

"First, I just want to say sorry Z." Jaxsyn leaned across the table and grabbed my hands. "You're my fuckin' sister and I should have loved you through your pain better. I've spoiled you. You've grown to expect certain shit from me and this time I dropped the ball when you needed me the most. We're grown but you're still my big little sister." She smiled through her watered eyes. "I never wanted to take Nevaeh from you Z. Never. I feel like every conversation we've had about that situation, you were the villain. I allowed you to be, but—"

"Jax, stop. I gave birth to a baby that I actually left at a hospital without even knowing what would happen next. We've already--"

"No." Jaxsyn rubbed the back of my hand. "I need to say this." Tears slid down her face and she took a deep breath. "You were messed up behind losing Nash. That man treasured the ground you walked on, and in a blink of an eye, he was gone. You were pregnant and had just lost the love of your life and the father of your unborn child. Sis, you were struggling emotionally, and I kicked you while you were down instead of doing everything in my power to lift you up. I can blame pregnancy emotions or everything that I had going on with Sih, but nothing should have kept me from holding you down during that time. The thought of losing Messiah shakes my whole soul so I can't even imagine the amount of pain you were going through. I should have done more. That's always been my job and like I said, the ball was dropped. I was so fuckin' hurt and angry that I reacted out of emotion instead of evaluating the bigger picture. For that, I'm extremely sorry." We both cried and I nodded my head. I love my sister to death, and I already knew she wasn't being-

"I killed Sandy last night." Sih blurted out, interrupting my thoughts and I gasped for the air that felt like it had been instantly snatched from my lungs.

"Sih." Jax shot a look his way and they stared at each other for a moment before turning to me. I'm quite sure my mouth was hanging wide open.

"It was no easy way to say it Z. She was in the back of the van with my daughter in her arms and talking shit. I did what needed to be done and I'm sorry that decision causes you pain." He apologized but had zero remorse, and I stood to walk away. I needed a minute.

"Zionna he," I held my hand up as I continued to walk out. I didn't need another explanation, his was fine. My mother helped start this bullshit, so I knew her fate. I know how Messiah and his people gets down but hearing it out loud was hard for me to swallow in this moment. She was a horrible mother most of the time and hearing Giz say that Rebecca paid her with drugs to keep me away from my father, made me hate her even more. My whole life she'd lied to me to keep me where she wanted me but at the end of the day, she was still my mother. I just didn't know how to feel.

"You busy?" I called my ex-boyfriend Quan. We were still on some friend shit and I appreciated it because I really just needed a friend right now.

"Nah. Just walked into the crib from work. You alright?"

"Not really. My mother is… gone."

"Damn, Z. Where you at? I'll come to you."

"I'm about to Uber to you if you don't mind. I don't want to be where I am, home, or alone."

"Come on."

"Thanks."

"No thanks needed. See you in a minute." We hung up and I ordered an Uber. I needed to clear my mind and I couldn't do it here and I would only drink myself into a stupor if I was alone.

****

I laid in Quan's arms crying for hours. The tears didn't start to flow until the liquor hit my system. He knew my struggle with alcohol, so he cut me off at one glass of wine, but I needed that shit so bad to take the edge off.

"Jax and I talk shit about all the bad times, but it wasn't all bad. This one Christmas my momma and Kabrina stole two bikes off of a Walmart truck with their crazy asses. Quan, the damn bikes weren't even put together yet, so we had to figure out how to assemble a bike with no tools, but we all did that shit together and had

65

so much fun doing it. They watched us ride around the basement while they drank their liquor and listened to their music. Kabrina had cooked so we laughed, joked, danced, ate good, and chilled. Shit felt… normal. That was one of the best Christmases that I've ever had." I wiped the tears that continued to fall. Sandy wasn't perfect by anyone's standards but knowing that she was gone for good seemed surreal. She's always been a pain in my ass, but she was my pain, a consistent pain that would no longer be around.

"You gon' be straight Z. You're one of the strongest women that I've ever known. Just like you said, all the times weren't bad so let the good memories ease your pain."

"Thanks, Quan."

"You're welcome." He kissed my forehead and I looked up at him.

"Why couldn't you be this guy for me, but you could be this guy for her?" I nodded my head towards his nightstand where a picture of him and his ex was still sitting.

"I was trying to make up for how bad I fucked up with you. The look you had on your face the day you told me about you and ol' boy crushed my ass. That shit fucked me up that we were really over and that I had hurt you so deeply that you found solace in another man's arms. My momma used to always say '*wait until that girl figures out she's being stupid for yo' raggedy ass, you gon' be sick*'. All the fuck I heard was her calling you stupid and I instantly jumped to your defense while missing the fact that she was warning me, and she was right. I was sick as fuck, but I saw it coming. I knew you deserved better so I couldn't stand in the way of that. I vowed that day, if I got serious about someone else, I would give them my all." He chuckled. "She was my karma though. She pulled a me on me and I couldn't do shit but take it and part ways. Bitch gave me a STD and the same day I found out, I went up to

66

her job to cuss her ass the fuck out but instead, caught her and her ex fuckin' in the car that I was paying the note on. I didn't even have shit to say. It was my karma, so I sat her shit outside, changed my locks, turned the volume up on the TV and watched ESPN until I fell asleep."

"I want to be happy that happened to you, but the pain and embarrassment you put me through is not something I would even wish on an enemy."

"I'm so fuckin' sorry Zionna. I was young and stupid, and then the shit just became something I did. Women were throwing the pussy at me and instead of me focusing on the loyal one that I had at home, I was weak and fell victim to my flesh. Never in a million years did I want to hurt you the way that I did Z. More than anything else, you were my best friend, and it still bothers me that I caused you any pain." He placed his index finger under my chin and made me look at him. "Can you ever forgive me?"

"For me, I forgave you a long time ago." I wiped my tears and as soon as I moved my hand he leaned in and kissed me. I moved my head back, shocked that he even attempted to kiss me, and he did it again. This time I felt his tongue inching between my lips and I opened my mouth to receive it. I leaned into him and allowed his kisses to get deeper. I didn't know what had come over me; maybe stress, maybe depression, could have been grief, but whatever it was, I allowed it and I didn't regret it. Although nothing is going to come from this, he felt like home and I needed to feel that in this moment.

Jaxsyn

Sih wasn't taking any more chances and he proved that to me the moment we pulled up to our home. He had our shit locked down like Fort Knox. He had his cousins and about thirty Knights spread out all over the grounds. Niggas posted with rifles and AK's, sharp shooters on the roof, and five big ass dudes standing guard on our front porch. I'm sure if I would have gone to the backyard, I would have found something similar. The shit was so official they were speaking into headsets to communicate with each other. "Prez and his family are entering the front door." I heard one of the big men whisper into his sleeve and I looked at Messiah who didn't seem phased at all.

We still had my whole family tagging along which meant they were in my home as well and I can't lie, I didn't know how to feel about that. I just couldn't trust them and knowing they were in my home where I'm supposed to feel the most peace, honestly bothered me. Messiah had this shit locked down with armor but what about the potential threats that was freely roaming around inside of our home. In my opinion they couldn't be trusted, and I wasn't about to let my guard down around them and allow some more bullshit to happen that we could have prevented. The days of freely trusting muthafuckas was done and over with.

This Rebecca shit really messed me up and now I'm running back different conversations we've had. I'm thinking about every moment I've spent with this bitch and wondering how much information was reported back to the enemy. She had been like a mother to me my whole life. I've always seen her as my protector and secret keeper. I trusted Rebecca with my life and would check the woman that gave birth to me, before I allowed her to disrespect

Rebecca. Now, I just felt stupid, like a pawn in a game that I didn't even know was being played.

I remember Kabrina used to always say, *'that bitch is phony as fuck, you'll see. You get one momma Jaxsyn Blackwell and I'm going to love you from my soul at my lowest and until my dying day. That bitch ain't gone spit on you if you're on fire. Watch what I tell you. Don't worry though, I'll be right there by your side to wipe your tears when she can no longer hide her horns because I'm momma, and that's what I'll always do.'* Her words have been on repeat in my head since we opened the doors to the cargo van that Rebecca was willingly sitting in the back of. Kabrina was right this whole time which made me wonder how much she actually knew or if she really just caught a vibe from Rebecca. I wanted to pick up my phone and ask but remembered Sandy's words.

I ran out of the room and straight into Messiah's arms. I looked up at him fighting my emotions because this man was tired, and bullshit was still stacking up against us. The last thing I needed was to add more to his already full plate. I had done that before, and he didn't deserve for me to do it again.

"Did Fresh say anything about Kabrina? I couldn't call last night because of the explosion."

"We're going to find her, baby." He kissed my head and stepped around me. His energy was off, and I knew the information about his father had fucked him up. We've had so many late-night conversations about how he hated his father for leaving him and Nash. For making them grow up faster than they should have. They were barely teenagers when they started hustling and even younger than that, trying to figure out how to survive on the unforgiving streets of New York. Their mother Charlene was trying to keep up appearances for people but she wasn't shit and it made Sih and Nash hate their father even more for not coming to save them. Then to find out that Mauricio didn't

69

even know about them was a lot for Messiah to take in. Especially considering Mauricio's status in this world. Their lives could have been completely different, but then again, his father was pretty much a pimp back in the day so maybe not *much* different.

I shook off my own feelings and went to find Giz. I told him I needed him to watch the girls and no one else was to come near them. I wanted him in the room with them until we got back, and he simply nodded and went straight upstairs to their room. Giz vibed with me like we were really family. I didn't have to say much for him to know exactly where I was coming from and I loved that about him. Blood couldn't make us more family than we already were.

"Come here baby." I grabbed Sih's hand before he could object and started walking. When we got to the garage, I grabbed his helmet, jacket, and his keys and passed them to him.

"I have shit to do, Jax."

"Yup. You sure do." I put my helmet and jacket on and hit the garage door opener. "And you'll do it when we get back." I patted the seat of his bike and he stared at me for a minute before getting on and then helping me on the back. He hadn't ridden his motorcycle since he came home, and I know when we first met, he told me that taking long rides on his bike was therapeutic for him. That's why him and Nash started The Knights years ago. I wanted him to have a sense of peace even in the midst of our storm and this was the perfect place to start. He's at his best when his mind is clear, and we have too much shit going on for his judgement to be clouded.

"Where to?"

"Just drive, handsome." I wrapped my arms around him, and he pulled off.

We rode around the city for an hour before we hit the freeway and ended up exactly where I knew we would.

Whenever he was overwhelmed or needed an escape, he would come to the park that he brought me to the first night we kicked it. He needed this right now and I knew he would eventually make his way here and it was even more perfect that we rode his motorcycle.

We got off the bike and walked over to the bench in front of the lake. I passed him a blunt from my cross-body purse and he smirked. We didn't say a word as he sparked it. The calm that I'd felt that very first night started to take over and ease some of my tension. The sun was going down and the scenery brought on a tranquil feeling. My son's absence was threatening to send me back into the darkest space in my mind again and I needed the serenity of this park just as much as Messiah did.

"I just keep thinking *why me*. You know?" He passed me the blunt while staring off. "Why the fuck, out of everybody in this world, was I chosen to struggle the way that I've struggled? Why did it have to be my brother... my fuckin' children? What did I do to have this weight placed on my shoulders? I ain't never fucked with nobody that didn't deserve to feel my wraith, I've never been no lyin' ass nigga, no hoe ass moves in my past, nothing. How is all this unwarranted shit resting on my back?"

"I feel the same way, Bae." I passed him the blunt and then got up and walked around the bench. I placed a few kisses on his neck then massaged his shoulders, trying to ease some of the tension that I could feel the moment I touched him. "Who the fuck said I wanted to grow up so fast? You know. I never even got the chance to be a kid because the grumbling from mine and my sister stomachs wouldn't allow me to be. Yeah, I could have went to my dad's house more but then I would have had to leave my sister alone, and that was never an option. Before I even hit double digits, I was playing the role of a provider and protector... Horrible adult decisions brought me face to

71

face with a nigga that had his fingers inside of my sister while her mother was laid out high as fuck two doors down. I was a kid catching my first body." This was my first time speaking on that situation out loud and tears streamed down my face. "So much shit happened back then, and to find out that it was all a part of a petty ass plot hurts deep. A plot that later lead to our babies getting snatched out of their home." I took a deep breath and we both remained quiet and caught up in our thoughts. I kept massaging his shoulders until every knot that I initially felt, was gone. I walked around the bench and kneeled down in front of him. Tears were silently sliding down his face and I wiped them. "We didn't deserve the lives that we were thrown into and the deck was stacked against us from the very start, Daddy, but we made it baby. Shit ain't perfect but we're here together and we're going to get our son back and hopefully my mother. You're going to give me the happiness you promised me and we're going to get our happily ever after. God gives his toughest battles to his strongest soldiers. I have to believe that. *We*, have to believe that. We got this, baby." I forced a smile and he looked up at me.

"My mafuckin' Tinkerbell," he said under his breath as he pulled me into a hug. "I love you so fuckin' much, baby."

"I love you too." We held each other and allowed the quiet to center us. Thoughts that had been running rampant before, were calming down and becoming clearer by the second. I could feel Messiah relaxing in my arms and that's what I wanted. It's what we needed so we could face this shit storm head on. He couldn't focus if his mind was running in a million different directions.

I loosened my grip on him and we backed away from each other slowly. I looked into those beautiful, brown eyes that I'd fallen in love with, and he was back. I could still see the wheels spinning but his vision wasn't clouded. I leaned forward and kissed him deeply. I couldn't

72

even remember the last time I kissed him so deeply and passionately. We both moaned from the overwhelming connection we shared. We should have still been making up for all the time we missed when he was in jail but instead, we were thrown into some bullshit that had us disconnected and off of our square. No matter how many positive affirmations we were kicking to ourselves and each other, the pain, anger, and confusion had been running us. We needed to plug back into each other and the situations that we were facing. This was our moment to do that, and what better place than where we connected for the first time.

I stroked the back of his head as our tongues intertwined, then slowly pulled my jacket off. His hands slid up my sides as he hooked my shirt on his fingertips, bringing it up. The only reason we broke our kiss was so that we could bring my shirt over my head and then we started again. His lips were like soft pillows and I couldn't get enough. I moved my right hand down and started stroking his dick. He was already hard as a rock and my body was begging for him. I could feel my juices spilling throughout my folds. My clit started to beat like a heart from sheer anticipation and desire. I had butterflies in my stomach as I broke our kiss again and stared into the eyes of the man I'm going to spend the rest of my life with. Never breaking our stare, we both slowly undressed. We didn't give a damn about being out in the open naked as the day we were born. The intimacy and love we shared was something I didn't even know existed, and in this moment, we were fully present for each other. I felt this man in my spirit. He was imprinted on my heart, and our souls tied, binding us together by something bigger than the both of us.

"Shit."

"Mmm."

The response that came from both of us proved just how much we needed to feel each other. His strong hands

73

wrapped around my tiny waist as he guided me all the way down. I whimpered as my head dipped back. The pain and pleasure combination that was happening made me wetter and he grunted. It's nothing sexier than a man willing to show his woman how good she's pleasing him. I rolled my hips sensually as I watched my baby's face contort from pleasure. His hands roamed up and down my back as he watched me take all of him in. Between his intense stare, and the groans he was making, my kitty was coating his dick with my cream.

Sih pulled me closer to him and covered my lips with his. Our breathing was heavy, but our kiss stayed slow and sensual. He stood without breaking our kiss and I wrapped my arms around his neck tighter, using it as leverage to continue riding him. He had other plans though. He tapped my leg and lifted me to slide himself out. My feet were placed on the ground and he turned me around. Before entering me, his kisses started at the back of my neck and then he slowly made his way down. The intimacy between us has always been unmatched and this time was no different.

"I love you Tink." He lifted my right leg and placed it on the bench as he leaned me forward.

"I love you too baby." I looked back at him and he smirked before looking down. His hands spread my ass open as he entered my kitty. I gripped the back of the bench and arched my back the way he taught me.

"Siiiih." I cried out from the pressure he was applying to my G-Spot damn near immediately. There was no mercy being given and he was driving deeper and deeper into my tunnel. His huge hands wrapped around my waist as he pulled me onto his dick, slamming into me at the same time. He was trying to commit a murder. My organs were slowly dying, and my legs started to tremble uncontrollably. "I'm... I'm... shiiiit baby."

"Yeah, I see it, Beautiful. Cum all over your dick, Ma." He said cockily causing me to look back at him again. He was biting down on his bottom lip and watching the show my body was putting on for him. My ass was in the air bouncing, legs like noodles, and my juices drenched us both. He pounded into me harder causing my pussy to contract around his swell. I started screaming as I came so hard, I almost gave myself a headache. He wasn't done with me yet though, he kept going.

Messiah had some making up to do. He picked me up again but this time I had no control. His left hand was under my leg and his right hand gripped my ass. Once again, murdering my middle. This time I could feel tears gathering in the wells of my eyes. The pleasure he was giving me was overwhelming. I wrapped my arms around him bringing our bodies closer. The skin-to-skin contact added to the euphoria surrounding us and my body jerked again letting us both know that I was cummin'. He stroked me with precision through my orgasm and then I felt him stiffen. I knew he was about to cum too, so with the little bit of energy left inside of me, I started milking him until he was weak. His throaty groan as he spilled inside of me was incredible and added to what I was already feeling. We both exhaled deeply and just like that, he was refocused, and I was miles away from my dark place.

"God hasn't brought us this far to just leave us." I whispered as I kissed his neck and he nodded, holding me tighter.

We were going to be okay, and I knew it in my heart of hearts.

Rebecca

I was going stir crazy in my hotel room. In twenty-four hours, I had lost everything that was ever important to me and I needed to come up with a plan to get it back or hell, at least some of it. I had lost my husband who regardless of my transgressions I love dearly, my children, Jax, my grandkids, my lover, and my stepson. This was not how this was supposed to happen.

Fernando and his other brother Jose wanted their youngest brother Mauricio, to pay for the disrespect he'd shown when their father passed the family business to Fernando. Granted, Mauricio was the first choice, but Fernando showed his ass about the decision that was made. Their father was sick and didn't have the energy to fight his oldest son, so he took the position from Mauricio and named Fernando as the head of the Cartel. From the stories I've been told, Mauricio didn't care one way or another. Fernando wanted his little brother to be more bothered than he was, and somehow took his lack of interest, as disrespect. He started doubling Mauricio's workload both in New York and Detroit. The goal was to prove that their father's initial decision was wrong. Every task that was thrown at Mauricio was completed with perfection, in a timely manner, and in most cases brought in more money than it had previously. Fernando's plan backfired and made him look worse.

Soon after that, Fernando's jealousy and anger couldn't be kept under wraps and he and Mauricio fell out completely. After they went their separate ways, Mauricio started doing his own thing in New York, then Miami, and both cities brought him wealth that surpassed even his own expectations. Fernando wanted him to fall flat on his ass and have to crawl back to him, but just the opposite happened. That sparked an anger inside of Fernando like nothing anyone had ever saw and then Mauricio went off the grid. Fernando has been searching and plotting on his brother since before I met him, and it all seemed ego driven and excessive. As soon as I spoke on Messiah and Nash, he lit up like a Christmas tree.

I had no idea mentioning their names in his presence would mean anything. I was simply telling him something about Jax and that's when I found out that he had a nephew that was already infiltrating the Knight's so he could make the sons of his arch nemesis pay for the sins of their father. Fernando said they had millions in liquid assets which meant they had even more that no one knew about. To him that was a dead giveaway that they were running their father's business. Once he shared that information with me, I could clearly see he was like a dog with a bone and the obsession was toxic.

Never in a million years did I suspect giving him the run down on Messiah and Nash every now and then would lead to Dominic and Ollie going after them and getting Nash killed. I felt so fucking responsible for that and the guilt only intensified as I held a crying and heartbroken Jaxsyn who bragged on how good of a person Nash was. Then Ollie was killed, and my soul was crushed. I've been around these boys since they were little. No one knew, but I was only a part-time therapist. I split my time between my home and Fernando's. His wife Karen had died a few years prior so when I came along, I helped fill a void. The connection was instant for the four of us, so hearing Dominic call me a bitch and tell me to refer to him as Gato broke my heart for multiple reasons.

My thoughts led me to call him, but the call went straight to voicemail. I was blocked. I shook my head and called Fernando. He picked up on the third ring and didn't say anything.

"If anyone in this world knows me and my heart, it's you. You're mad because we lost Ollie and the mere thought of losing another son is gut wrenching, but you know me, Fernando. I didn't want to leave our son baby and had my life not been flashing before my eyes, I wouldn't have. I didn't even get to the end of the block before I started calling for help. I've wiped his tears and runny nose, I've kissed his boo-boos and tucked him in at night, I've prayed over our boys and-" I couldn't control my emotions. I loved the three of them just as much or possibly more than the husband and children I had at home. Leaving them and going back to two sons that were attached to their father like glue, and two whiny spoiled ass daughters who were equally attached to Brian was miserable sometimes. I think that's why my bond with Jaxsyn grew as deep as it did. She longed for a mother so when she came over, she was attached to me and I needed that. That's what I got from Fernando, Dominic, and Ollie. They hadn't had a woman in the house since Karen, and when I came in, they appreciated me more than I could have ever imagined.

"Come home." Fernando hung up and I took a deep breath. Those words were music to my ears, and I hopped up. I couldn't live without him and I hoped he could feel my words because I meant them.

****

I spent the whole morning on my knees making up with Fernando. I could tell he was still pissed off, but I couldn't tell whether it was at me, or the situation that we found ourselves in. I found out five of his men were taken from Messiah's grandmothers house and he couldn't be sure whether they were dead or alive and talking. He couldn't take any chances so plans that were already in place before, had to be scrapped and he was right back at square one, only this time he didn't have anyone on the inside like before. At this point, the only advantage he had was my grandson. He was going to kill Junior and send the video to Messiah to get into his head. Fernando had become desperate to find out Mauricio's location and breaking down Messiah mentally seemed like the best decision, but I begged him to come up with another plan. I had no idea whether he was going to listen or not but at least I'd tried. I had to. He hates that I love them so much but that didn't change overnight. My babies were innocent and before I gave him and Dominic the layout of Messiah and Jaxsyn's home, I made that very clear. The kids were only supposed to be used for bargaining, nothing else. I felt nauseated at the fact that he was even considering touching Junior to harm him. Shit was so out of hand right now.

"Fuck." He released and I swallowed every last drop. I stroked his balls and he started getting hard again. I got up and tried to climb on top of him like I normally would, but he pushed me away. Again. "Go make my dinner."

"Fernando."

"You're back Rebecca, be happy with that." He walked away. I didn't know how to feel but I got dressed and went down to the kitchen.

Twenty minutes later the doorbell chimed and before I could dry my hands to go get it, Smitty was opening the door. It was a tall blonde woman that was half dressed, well maybe not even half. If she sneezed too hard her titties and ass would have definitely been exposed.

"Mr. Vargas called me."

"Right this way."

"Called her for what?" I asked Smitty and he kept walking towards the basement, but she childishly made a gesture with her hands like she was sucking dick and I wanted to burst into tears. He's never disrespected me before so instead shedding the tears that I so desperately wanted to shed, I ran upstairs to where I had just left Fernando.

"Son, he's not going to lose thirty million in product and supplies and send someone else to handle it. Keep a look out at that warehouse in Georgia and kill everything moving around him as soon as he arrives. Grab him and bring his ass to the estate. I need to find my brother and he's going to lead me straight to him. This is the closest we've ever been so don't fail me."

"I won't, my insider is keeping me up to date. You know I'm normally all about playing with muthafuckas, but he had a hand in killing Ollie and I'm ready to end his ass. I damn sure won't fail."

"Good. If shit goes left out there, we'll kill his fuckin' son so he can feel my pain and then those other kids are next. Eventually we'll kill his bitch in front of him until he gives us everything we want. Whatever it takes my boy."

"Now that's what I'm talking about. Let's crank this shit up a notch or two." They laughed.

"Alright son, I'm about to slide into something, so call me when you have him."

"I thought you weren't fuckin' with Rebecca like that?"

"She's here but I'm not. She still has a bond with Messiah's bitch. That relationship may come in handy again, so I need to keep her close for now. I just called Kitty over here to scratch this itch, so I'm not even tempted to touch Rebecca." They both laughed again as tears raced to my chin. He was playing me. I gave him all of me and he was fuckin' playing *me*. No way, I pulled my phone out before he even ended his call.

Me: *Gato's father name is Fernando Vargas and he's behind everything. If you're going to Georgia, it's a setup and they have someone on the inside. I don't know* *who. Fernando is becoming desperate, and I don't know how much longer I can protect Junior but I'll do my best.*

Messiah: *This changes nothing. You're dead to us!!*

Me: *I know... I heard...*

"Hey." I smiled as I walked into Fernando's office cutting the laugh that he was having at my expense short.

"I'll call you back son." He hung up. "What?"

"I was wondering if I can see my grandson? I know you hate for me to call them that but they're my grandkids, baby, and I miss them. We already know I'll never be able to see the other ones, so can I at least see him?" He stared at me and gave a slow nod. The look in his eyes let me know he wasn't just talking shit to Dominic, he actually felt that way. The love had been replaced by disgust and it was too obvious to ignore. Crazy thing is, I've given my all to them for years and one split second mistake that was out of my control had them tossing me out like yesterday's trash. That made me question everything. The look on his face made me want him dead.

"I'll have Smitty bring you to him. We'll let you know when."

"Thanks baby." I went to kiss him, and he turned his head as he got up.

"Go finish cooking dinner while I handle this business real quick."

"What business?"

"Don't fuckin' question me Rebecca. Go do what the fuck I just told you to do." I shook my head and went back to the kitchen as he went straight to the basement. My life was happening in moments and each one was blowing my mind. I went from dying to be back in Fernando's arms and praying that God would allow him to forgive me, to hating his very existence.

Me: *I'm going to text you an address as soon as I get to it, so be ready to move fast because it'll be where Junior is located.* I deleted the message and finished cooking dinner as different scenarios ran through my head. I wasn't about to allow Fernando to use me not one more second. Because of him I had a target on my back that I was completely fine with until he showed his true colors. I had to figure some shit out and I couldn't do it in this house. He needed to hurry up with his whore so I could get the hell on and go see my grandson. I needed space to come up with a plan to rid the world of this monster and his son. Gone was the rose-colored glasses and I wanted them handled accordingly. After all, according to Gato, I'm nothing more than the bitch they shared memories with.

Messiah

I sat in my brothers living room where we'd shared countless moments and created more memories than I could count, just staring at this text from Rebecca. As soon as I saw her name pop up earlier, my skin crawled. This bitch had to have a death wish contacting me, but then I read her words over and over. She confirmed what I already knew about the warehouse in Georgia, which is why I stopped Lace from going back out there earlier. After she talked to Fresh, they planned to fly out there to get shit situated, but I knew these niggas were trying to lure me out, even though I wasn't hiding. I also knew someone on the inside was working with them because my shipments are untouchable. Nash and I were too smart to ever get caught slipping so someone had to be feeding them information, it was only a matter of time before I found out who.

I continued to stare at the text, allowing my hate for Rebecca to run freely. This bitch sat in my fuckin' face giving me her condolences and comforting my woman, knowing she had a hand in my brother's demise. Rebecca is the worst kind of snake. The kind of snake that remind you of why you can't trust muthafuckas. Rebecca chose her fate when she crossed her family many years ago. This bitch chose to slither in the dirt with snakes so I'm going to return her to that same dirt she's been slithering in.

My head snapped around at the sound coming from behind me and I had my gun aimed and ready.

"It's just me. Don't kill me like you did my mother." Zionna held her hands up and I lowered my weapon.

"Man, come on with all that. You know what she did, and you know if it was any other way, it would have played out differently. I fuck with you the long way Z, you're my sister, I wouldn't purposely do shit to hurt you."

"Just shut up because I wanna be mad and you're making it hard." She plopped down next to me and passed me the blunt she was smoking. "I know you did what you had to do. This shit hurt though, and I don't even know why. For the first time, in a long time, I thought about the good times we've shared, and I got emotional. It's like she wanted to be better, and I could see that shit sometime when she thought I wasn't paying attention, but something was always holding her back. The drugs numbed her, but she's never told me what lead her down the dark path she took. Why did she need to numb herself? I wanted to understand her, and she never gave me that chance. I feel robbed. Why wasn't I good enough for her to do better?" I passed the blunt back and shook my head. I didn't have an answer for her, but that shit hit close to home in more than one way. Jax and I had just talked about this. Shit, my momma's been choosing the streets over me and my brother and chasing random men, my whole life. She partied, drank, smoked, and did drugs with strangers every single day, like she didn't have two boys at home waiting for her. I remember me and Nash was like four and five or some shit and she left us in the house for two weeks to go on vacation with some nigga she had just met. That was the first time my granny took us.

"Man, who the fuck knows why our parents did the shit that they did. You can't waste your time worrying about the mistakes and missteps of other people Z. All you can do is forgive her for your own sanity and strive to be a better person than she was."

We sat quietly for a minute in our own thoughts. "When I moved to Arizona, I was still drinking. I didn't go to rehab like I said I was going to do." Zionna paused. "I fuckin' loved him Sih." She broke down crying and I held her in my arms as she cried from her soul. The howl that came from her was painful to hear. Nash was missed and we've all been wrapped up in bullshit that none of us got the chance to properly mourn him. "He loved me through my flaws and all bro. I was broken when I met Nash and his presence alone was so big that he healed me without even knowing." She gasped.

"He loved yo' ass too. Everything was my baby this and my baby that. What y'all had was special and for a purpose. Maybe him healing you was his last task and then he was called home." She raised her head and stared at me.

"My sister is lucky to have you. That was powerful and I needed it."

"I'm the lucky one and we both know it." We laughed. "You gon' be straight Z. I promise. Stop trying to drown your pain with alcohol and weed. That's no different than Sandy numbing her pain with crack. Feel that shit and then start healing. Nashon was that nigga and it ain't a day that go by that I don't miss him but it ain't a day that go by that I don't try to make him proud. Don't let him down Zionna, he's always wanted what was best for you."

"I already did. I left our fuckin' daughter in a hospital alone without knowing her fate." She continued to cry, and I allowed her to. Shit, she did that and she needed to feel it. That's a decision that she's going to have to come to grips with on her own. "I also kissed my ex today too. The same ex that he warned me not to deal with. I feel stupid as hell right now. Things would have escalated past that point but Alyssa called me crying so I stopped it. I just--"

"Crying for what?"

She shook her head. "Apparently she's pregnant and the guy is married. His wife has been harassing her but doesn't know Lyss is pregnant yet. I think, I'm not sure. She was crying so hard it was difficult to hear her. He's been lying to her or something. Plus, she's depressed because Jax ain't fuckin' with her, she needs help coping with all this shit."

"The doctor that did Jax ultrasound before I went in?"

"I have no clue who the doctor is or if he's the same guy she's pregnant by. She's supposed to be meeting me here in an hour. This is Jax department. I don't even know what the hell to say to her."

"Just be an ear." I started grabbing my phone and keys. "My bad about coming here. I know this yo' shit now but I just feel closer to him here."

"Boy bye. Come anytime. I'll be leaving as soon as we find Junior and Kabrina, so you'll have free reign."

"You still going back?"

"Yeah... Too much has happened here for me to find peace in Detroit."

"Peace is wherever you allow it to be Z. I'll get up with you later sis. Tell Alyssa to call me if she needs me." With that I walked out so I could tell Jax about this text Rebecca sent and get with Giz, it's time I sit down with Mauricio and hear him out.

Alyssa

Kevin's wife called my phone thirteen times and left a message each time. When she couldn't get my attention that way, she started leaving messages on social media. I guess she was pissed about him leaving their home and coming to be with me, but she should take that up with him. I've tried to leave Kevin alone several times, but he won't allow me to. He's in love and when I walk away, he tracks me down every single time and begs me to stay. I love him too, so it's never a question as to whether I want to stay or not.

I've tried to respect their marriage, but I can't respect it more than he does. Neither of us planned for things to get this out of hand or for her to get hurt, especially him. I was supposed to be something young and fun to do and he ended up falling in love and now he's stuck between a rock and a hard place. He's greedy and I take responsibility for allowing it to get this far but it snuck up on me too. Now we're expecting a baby and own a condo together. There was no turning back from the decisions we chose to make at this point.

I called and told him about Mrs. Messer harassing me and he apologized repeatedly and came right over. He witnessed the drama that I go through with this woman firsthand. My phone was going off with notifications and calls until he powered it off. No number of apologies would make me feel better. Of course he resorted to sex, which was his go to apology, but when I woke up he was in the bathroom whispering. I got up and went to stand outside the door because obviously if he's whispering, it's for a reason.

"Baby I've told you over and over that I'm at work in the bathroom. Look at my clothes Heather. I'm not with her and I haven't been."

"I just can't trust you anymore Kevin. Do you think I want to have you FaceTime me every day, all day, just so I can believe what comes out of your mouth? Just so I know you're where you promised to be. You've turned me into this kind of woman Kevin, and I hate it." She started crying.

"I can't apologize enough baby. She meant nothing to me, and I haven't touched her in months. I promised you I wouldn't, and I haven't, baby. I can't lose you Heather and I've been proving to you that it's only you since you found out."

"Yeah, since I found out from a friend. You've embarrassed me in front of everyone, and for what? To play around with a kid that's our daughters age? If your mother was still alive, what would she think of the embarrassment you've brought to our home, to this family? I'm trying Kevin, I swear I am, but this is too much sometimes. I called that child so many times today it's ridiculous. I can't sleep at night and she probably sleeps perfectly fine knowing she's been with my husband as many times as she wanted."

"Come on Heather, we're in therapy, I'm home anytime I'm not working, we're taking more vacations, our sex life is back to where it used to be, and I actually enjoy you FaceTiming me during the day. I get to see your beautiful face." This motherfucker was such a liar. He told me that she knew everything about us and since she couldn't cope with him cheating, they had been talking about getting a divorce. His ass has been in therapy this whole time trying to work it out and they're having sex which he claimed they hadn't done since she found out. He supposedly was sleeping in their guest bedroom most nights. He even went as far as asking me to massage his back because the bed in the guest room was uncomfortable. I was pissed and petty. I barged in the bathroom and he damn near dropped the phone, but I caught it in midair. I looked dead at the camera while I swatted him away.

"He's a fuckin' liar! He left your home this morning because I called, and whenever I call, he comes running. We made love before he went to work and when I called to tell him you were harassing me, he left work and came running to me again. We're expecting a baby and we share a condo that's in both of our names. That's where we currently are. He's wearing his white coat but he's naked." I turned the camera around to the mirror we were facing and showed her that I was completely naked, and his dick was swinging from under his white coat. I turned the camera back around and her face was saturated in tears. "I'm young and had a lapse in judgment. I never meant to hurt you and I know that sounds like complete and utter bullshit, but it's the truth. It also didn't help that he told me he was divorcing you, but from what I just heard that's just another lie to keep us both where we are. I'm done and you don't have to stay up worrying about me. I shouldn't have been dealing with his trash ass to begin with, but I am keeping my baby, that's what y'all both need to know." I tossed his phone that he wanted so bad at him and then stormed out of the bathroom. He was playing both of us and I can't lie and say it didn't hurt. He didn't have to lie to me. There was no need. His commitment was to her, so there was no reason to sell me a dream when all we were doing is having sex. No one told him to tell me he loved me and that he wanted to make us official. Even with the baby on the way, I know what this is between us. He didn't have to move the way he did, and I wasn't about to be the only one hurting in this equation.

I slipped into my clothes, grabbed my keys, purse, and phone and darted out of the front door. I didn't want to even look at Kevin. I wanted to call Jax so bad, but she hates me and that wasn't changing anytime soon. Sydnee was too young to understand what I was going through or to give me any advice, so I called Zionna. Just hearing her voice had me emotional. Thankfully she told me to meet her at her house. She'll never know just how much I appreciated her in this moment. Without my mother or Jax I felt lost but thank God Z and I started building a relationship, now I have another person in my support system.

"I can help you pump that sweetheart. You're too pretty to be out here smelling like gas."

I turned around and smiled. "Thank you but I got--" He pulled a gun out and my smile dropped immediately.

"Nah, I got it." He walked up on me and took the nozzle out of my gas tank. I started shaking from pure fear and he smirked.

"Did your grown ass just piss on yourself?" He busted out laughing as we both looked down and I had. As soon as I saw that gun, my thoughts went to my baby and I panicked. His phone rang and he looked down. I wanted to use that opportunity to run but again, fear washed over me, and I thought about him shooting me in the back so I stayed right where I was.

"Yeah. I got her. Her sneaky ass doesn't know she just traded her grandson for her daughter but she will soon… Everything is go, we're ready. Yeah, I took care of that too… Okay, cool." He hung up and rubbed the side of my face. "Bring your pissy ass on." He started walking away like he dared me to do anything other than what he said. I slowly followed since I had no other option. "I was going to let you ride in the car but now you have to get in the trunk pissy girl."

"What?"

"You wanna get in there on your own or you want me to put you in there? The choice is yours."

"Why are you doing this to me?" I was crying so hard I could barely breathe. This day couldn't get any worse.

"Thank your mother for your demise sweetheart. She fucked with the wrong ones and now you're about to be a lesson that she has to learn," he said as he nodded towards the trunk. Once again, my mother had put me in a situation that I was completely oblivious about. I was going to die over her bullshit and that reality hit me so hard I could barely breathe. I started hyperventilating and he didn't give a damn. He pushed me in the trunk so hard I busted my head on something going down. "I'm not trying to hear all that shit so shut the fuck up before I shoot you now." He slammed the trunk, and darkness surrounded me.

Jaxsyn

My adrenaline was pumping, and my heart was racing. My palms were sweaty, and my stomach was jittering. I didn't know what the hell was going on, but we were flying down the freeway and I had a million thoughts about the different scenarios that could have caused this.

As we pulled up, tears welled in my eyes. The first house that I've ever bought was on fire and far past the point of salvaging it. I had been trying to sell it since my divorce was finalized but I could honestly admit I had been dragging my feet about it. Not only did this house hold memories that were near and dear to me, but it was my first big girl purchase. I was proud of my house and the hard work that went into me getting it.

"Yeah, okay bitch... I hear you, but just know that I know, you only over there talkin' that big mouth shit because I'm cuffed, hoe." I heard a woman yelling and it caused me to turn around. She was cuffed like she said and sitting on the curb across the street from my home. I watched for a moment before Messiah guided me to where the detectives stood congregating with each other as the fireman battled my blazing home.

"I'm Jaxsyn Blackwell, the homeowner. Can any of you tell me how this happened?" All I knew is that one of them called me and told me the house was on fire and I needed to get down there as soon as possible.

"Hi Ms. Blackwell, I'm Detective Kilbourne." He extended his hand, and I shook it. "Do you know this young lady to the right of me?" He asked causing both me and Sih to look at the woman that was still yelling and going in on the young white officers standing in front of her. They weren't fazed in the least bit, but she was still laying into their asses relentlessly.

"No." I turned my attention to him and now all the detectives were looking at me.

"Well, she's the one who set the house on fire. You sure you don't know her?"

"I'm positive. She doesn't even look familiar." I looked back in her direction and our eyes locked. She busted out laughing and reared back, playfully kicking her feet in front of her.

"Heeeeey wifey," she said to me and my brows furrowed. "Thank your husband for these flames bitch! If Black thinks for one second that he's going to keep my daughter away from me so he can play house with your dead pussy havin' ass, he has another thing coming. I'll burn this bitch down again before I allow that to happen. Tuh."

"This bitch can't be serious." Sih shook his head. We had a million other things that we could have been taking care of but here we stood, in front of my burning home, getting yelled at by my ex-husband's thot ass baby momma who was loud and wrong.

"I've been divorced from him for two years because he has a boyfriend. What the fuck are you even talking about? You burned down my shit over a nigga that I don't even fuck with? He hasn't lived in this house in well over a year because I had him evicted!" I threw my hands up and shook my head. Her whole demeanor changed, and she looked demonic.

"He what?"

"You heard what the fuck I said. He has a boyfriend and we're divorced. It was his boyfriend that actually told me about you when you were pregnant. You did all this shit for nothing."

"Nah... Not for nothing." Her eyes went past me and before anyone could react, she hopped up off the curb effortlessly and took off running. That's when I noticed Black had walked up. His boyfriend Ty was with him, and before he could wrap his mind around the sight before him, she head butted the fuck out of him causing blood to gush from his mouth and nose, and her head. I gasped and covered my mouth. The police tackled her crazy ass like they were on a football field and she was on the opposing team. She was going the fuck off and didn't give two fucks about their knees in her neck and back. She called Black everything, but the child of God and I can't say he didn't deserve it. I had spazzed on him the same way so I couldn't judge her. Well, I could because the bitch slept with my husband, knowing he was married and burned my fuckin' house down, but I couldn't judge her for reacting to his lies. I didn't know what their pillow talk was like and niggas are great liars.

"You know you have to be bat shit crazy to use your face as a weapon like that." Sih chuckled and some of the officers joined in. I knew the wrath of Black's decisions and lies so I didn't find it funny. Her raw emotions after hearing me say we had been divorced was written all over her face but when I mentioned him having a boyfriend too, that was the straw that broke the camel's back. He had her in the dark and I knew that feeling all too well. She was young and dumb, and he probably sold her his best lies because you don't just pull moves like this over nothing. "Aye, we gotta roll." Sih looked up from his phone and grabbed my hand just as Black and Ty came walking up. His face was oozing blood and I didn't feel bad for him at all. I'm not pressing charges against her and I hope she gets out and does more shit to his ass.

"I'm sorry about all of this J."

"Boy fuck you and you." I rolled my eyes at both him and Ty. He was nothing more to me than another snake that I had to cut out of my life. If that nigga's mouth was open most likely a fuckin' lie was coming out of it and I didn't want to hear shit from him. Especially an apology for some shit he caused the moment he stepped outside of our marriage and entertained her young ass. Why apologize now? I hope she bring his ass nothing but drama and stress. He deserved that karma for the way he played with my heart.

We hopped in the car and Sih pulled off crazily in front of the police and they didn't even look twice. They must have been on payroll. "We on our way… Yup, surround that whole bitch. Alright bet." He hung up and dipped in and out of traffic and once he was back on the freeway, he glanced over at me. "Rebecca sent the address. Everybody gon' meet us over there."

"Everybody? Who's at the house with my babies? I don't want them alone with my siblings. Sih, I don't trust them. Jagger and Dawson have been too quiet, and I haven't saw Sydnee since we came home. They could be plotting, baby, please take me home." Tears streamed down my face instantly and he reached for my hand.

"Not them, Tink. Everyone that was at the house before we left is still there baby. I promise. The girls are safe, and our shit is locked down from the inside out and vice versa, but if you still want to go home, I can shoot you there real quick." I thought about his words for a moment and then shook my head no. I wanted to go with him. I wanted to be the first face my son saw if he was even at this location. We had talked about the probability that Rebecca was setting us up and we all knew that it was highly likely. This was the same bitch who set all this shit into motion with a man that she's been fuckin' with for years behind my father's back. Of course, it was suspicious that she all of a sudden had a change of heart. That's not how shit works. Either way we had to go though. Getting my son back was our main priority and if there was even the smallest possibility that he was at the address she texted to us, then we had to check it out. No doubt about it.

We pulled up to the address and a Range Rover was parked in the driveway. The windows were tinted dark so we couldn't see inside. Sih grabbed his phone from the cup holder and called Giz. He answered on the first ring and his voice came through the car speaker.

"Aye, they in this bitch and it's just Rebecca and the guy that brought her here. They've been arguing since they arrived. Apparently, Fernando is fuckin' somebody else and Rebecca is hurt about that shit. Since they're distracted with her drama, we can enter through the back door and set this bitch off."

"I'm looking at a side door too. I want six teams formed immediately for each entrance. Three teams stay outside guarding the exit while the rest of us rush in. Have Fresh meet me at the side door and you go through the back. Tell Reggie come around front. If my son ain't in here we're still taking both of they asses. Be careful because you know these niggas walking around with rocket launchers and shit, they could be anywhere, and up to anything. Necks on swivel."

"I got Knights canvassing the area too. This shit ain't going down like it did at granny house." Giz hung up and we both checked our guns for ammo and got out with no words spoken. We were on a mission and it wasn't shit to say. We were locked and loaded and ready to risk it all for our baby boy.

On the count of three we all busted in and since we were at the side door, we walked into the small hall that lead to the basement, and to the right of us Giz was coming through the kitchen door. None of us were near the front where we knew Rebecca was. Giz gave Sih a nod as him and the rest of the team went running through the house checking shit.

"Come on." Messiah and I raised our guns as we crept down the stairs leading to the basement. My heart was pounding out of my chest as the smell of piss, shit, sewer, and death invaded my nostrils. I prayed with each step we took, that my son was safe, and it wasn't his body decaying that I smelled. "Oh my God!" I yelled as my foot hit the concrete basement floor. My momma was laid out in a puddle of her own blood with a needle lying next to her arm as my son sat next to her with a plastic sword hanging over his granny like he was protecting her. I dropped to my knees and yelped. The pain that shot through me looking at both of them was something I couldn't even put into words if I tried. I crawled over to them and Junior reached for me.

"Mommy is so sorry baby." I went to grab him, and my mother started going crazy. My mind had been questioning whether she was dead or not and this moment answered all my prayers. We were praying so hard that Junior was here, and Rebecca wasn't on more bullshit and turns out, God had stepped in and showed out.

"Don't touch him. Don't touch my baby. Leave him alone." Kabrina was pulling on him and he laid on her chest with his sword gripped tightly in his little hands.

"It's me momma. It's Jaxsyn." I touched her and her head slowly turned. Her eyes were dazed, and she was obviously high as a kite. Her hair was soaked in fresh and dried blood causing it to stick to the floor. She gave me a weak smile and tried to reach for me like my son did.

"What did you call me?" She said in a raspy voice and I smiled.

"Girl." Tears poured from my eyes and I bent down and kissed her head. "I called you momma and I'll never call you anything else. I'm so sorry I ever did."

"I can die peacefully now." Her eyes closed and I started shaking like I was having a fuckin' seizure.

"Ma, no. Please momma don't do this!" I yelled and my son raised his head. He looked weak and Sih picked him up and started barking orders for them to get my mother to the hospital. There was no telling how many drugs or what kinds of drugs they had pumped her full of, but I just prayed that she didn't die. Messiah helped me up and I hugged him and our son. I was so complete in this moment.

"We gotta get the fuck out of here." Giz yelled and we darted up the stairs and out the side door. They put Rebecca and the guy she was arguing with in an unmarked van and sped off in the opposite direction. Reggie put my mother in his car, Giz hopped in another, and we ran to our car just as a helicopter started circling the house way lower than it should have been.

"Man, what type of shit is these niggas on now?" Messiah said as we pulled off.

"The type of shit that give muthafuckas nightmares." We both looked at each other and then in the backseat because neither of us said that shit. "I bugged the car. You can stop looking around stupidly. I told y'all you couldn't hide from me." Gato laughed as his voice boomed through the speakers of Sih's car. This nigga was next level crazy, and I could see Messiah's jaw tightening and the veins in his neck starting to protrude. Once again Gato was ten steps ahead of us and playing games.

"Man, what the fuck do y'all niggas want? I'm sick of this bullshit."

"Simple. Mauricio Vargas. Tell us where he is?"

"I don't even know that nigga. Y'all doing all this extra shit for nothing."

He laughed. "If you haven't noticed, little cousin, I'm no amateur. Don't feed me no bullshit because then I might get mad and remember that y'all killed my little brother and then shit is really going to get messy."

"An eye for an eye, my nigga."

"Nah. I don't play fair." *Tink... Tink... Tink...* bullets started bouncing off of our car and the helicopter got lower and lower, helping his aim. The lack of trees in this deserted ass area made us an easy fuckin' target which made me think Rebecca may have had a hand in this as well. He was right over us and there wasn't shit we could do and nowhere we could hide. I covered Junior's head hoping if a bullet penetrated the car, it would hit me instead. "Here, I think you forgot something."

We both looked at each other and all of a sudden something dropped from the helicopter making Messiah slam on his breaks and swerve, causing a train reaction. Giz slammed right into the back of us and I'm sure Reggie slammed into him. Our car went spinning out of control and before we hit the light pole I saw us barreling towards, my instincts were to hold my son as tight as possible. Closing my eyes, I tried to brace myself for the impact we couldn't avoid.

Zionna

The return call that I was waiting on from Alyssa never came, and it wasn't until I was in the car with Shawn and Fresh that I learned why. Gato had sent them a text message saying that Rebecca crossed the wrong one and my little sister was going to pay for it. She was tied up and beaten and it crushed me, especially because she's pregnant. I had just talked to her and she was so distraught and now this. She couldn't catch a break but none of us could. Every step we took forward we got knocked right back to the starting point.

Shawn and Fresh never told me where we were going when they came and got me, they just told me to get in the car. At this point I already knew not to question them. If they said move it was time to move. We had way too much going on to be giving them any shit when my safety or the safety of others could be at stake. I grabbed my purse and hopped my ass in the car.

When we pulled up to the hospital, I just knew Alyssa had been found, and that's why we were there. Never in a million fuckin' years did I expect the news that I got and before I could hit the ground, my father and Fresh caught me. This stupid fuckin' lunatic Gato dropped Sydnee from a helicopter, and she might not ever walk or talk again. She was pretty much mush, connected to a ventilator that was keeping her alive. From what they said, damn near every bone in Syd's body was broken. It's a surprise that she was even still barely breathing. Messiah hit a pole trying to avoid running her over and Jaxsyn and Junior went flying through the windshield. Jax's body was found sixteen feet from the crash. She had a head injury that they weren't giving us any information on but according to my dad, she had been in surgery for hours. Junior had a broken leg, and Messiah just had minor bruises and scrapes. Then there was poor Kabrina, she was barely hanging on like Sydnee. They were scared she wouldn't even make it through the next forty-eight hours. She had a cocktail of drugs in her system so strong that it could have knocked out a horse. Thank God she was in the house with Junior and was found in time to at least have a shot at fighting for her life… This shit was all bad.

The lobby was filled with tears and confusion. We were at war, and for what? These niggas were coming at us hard as fuck and they always seemed to be a step ahead. They knew Rebecca was giving up the location to where Junior was being held, and one up'd her by taking both Sydnee and Alyssa as retaliation for betrayal. Come to find out, Sydnee had reached out to Rebecca because she didn't believe she was capable of doing what we all said she did, unfortunately she had to learn the hard way that her mother wasn't as perfect as she assumed she was. The bitch was definitely dirty and everyone that she claimed to love was suffering because of it.

I can't lie, having my dad hold me in his arms felt amazing. I'd longed for this moment and although the situation wasn't ideal, knowing that everything my mother had told me about him loving his white family more than me was a legit lie, made this moment everything. He rubbed my head as I cried about my sisters and this whole situation and his love for me felt so genuine that it caused me to cry even harder.

"I love you so much, baby. We're going to be okay no matter what." He said, trying to convince us both.

"I love you too, daddy." His body stiffened and then he kissed my forehead repeatedly and I felt his tears falling on me. Never had I told him I loved him or called him anything but his first name. That's who he's always been but knowing the truth wouldn't allow me to go any further

101

with denying him my love, affection, or respect. I was outright mean over the years and he never gave up on me or treated me differently and for that, I'll spend the rest of my life showing the only parent I had left just how much I love and appreciate him.

After an hour of sitting in the lobby not knowing anything, the doctor that put Junior's leg in a cast came down and told us we could all finally go up to see him. The nurse that directed us there said someone would come to Junior's room with updates about Jax and Syd as soon as possible. My dad asked about Kabrina and they said he could go see her when he wanted. We all walked into the room and Messiah was lying with Junior, looking like Sih One and Sih Two, causing us all to smile. His little cast broke our hearts, but we had him back and that was all that mattered. Dad stayed for about twenty minutes and then rushed off to check on Kabrina. His ass was itching to get over there, but he needed to check on his grandson too. As soon as Messiah told us everything was fine with Junior, Dad jetted.

"I just gave Gizmo the room number, he on his way up." Fresh said as he took a seat next to me. I swear I wasn't trying to look at Nash's cousin the way that I was, but Lord have mercy this man was all kinds of fine. Sexy, smooth chocolate skin, chestnut brown eyes, low cut fade with a lineup that was done by a damn hair surgent. His body was solid, and his arms bulged but he wasn't bulky. Their whole family had nice ass rock hard bodies, but he wasn't buff like Giz. Giz is the kind of person you see in the gym and you're like "okay show off, you won already go sit the fuck down somewhere." He's the only one like that though, the rest are just sexy as fuck and they all come in different shades of yumminess.

"Wow," I said as the door opened, and Messiah's father walked in. No introduction was necessary. We used to joke about Nash and Sih looking like twins, now Junior is a mini version of them, but this shit here was copy paste level.

"He wouldn't take no as an answer." Giz came in and went straight to Junior and kissed his head. "Man, it's good to see this lil nigga here." Him and Messiah dapped each other and tapped their chest twice. My eyes watered thinking about all the times that I watched Sih do that with Nashon.

"Mauricio." His father extended his hand towards Sih and he shook it with no hesitation.

"Messiah." Mauricio nodded and looked at Junior with nothing but love. He rubbed his head and took a deep breath.

"Inadvertently I'm responsible for what's happening to you and your family. I haven't laid eyes on my brother for almost twenty years. His problem with me lies in his head and unfortunately that's spilled over into your world. I apologize. He's taken one of my children away and I won't allow him to take another, or anyone else. Consider this handled."

"This is personal now. I'm out for blood and I ain't gon' be able to rest until I have that muthafuckas blood on my hands. I appreciate the offer though."

"Well, we can handle him and his people together. This is personal for me too. You mind if I sit?" Messiah nodded towards the chair as he pulled Junior back into his arms and laid back.

Waiting around quietly was driving us all stir crazy. Giz was in and out making phone calls, I couldn't stop pacing the floor, Fresh was tapping a pen on the windowsill annoying the hell out of me, Shawn was flipping his phone in the air with his head leaned against the wall, Mauricio was bouncing his leg up and down, and Messiah was staring off into space, probably with a million scenarios running through his head.

"Hello. I'm Dr. Oswald. Is this Jaxsyn Blackwell's family?"

"Yes, we are." I ran over to her as Messiah climbed out of the bed. "I'm her sister and this is her husband. How is she?"

"Mrs. Blackwell has a very long road ahead of her. She has a diffuse axonal injury which means the trauma to her head caused her brain to move. During surgery, she had two seizures and her brain started to swell so we had to remove a piece of her skull." I stumbled back into Messiah and he held me up, but I could feel him shaking and it brought on the tears that I was trying to control.

"What?" Sih's voice was barely above a whisper and his cousins surrounded him.

"That sounds much worse than the reality of it. This definitely has the potential to have several different outcomes, but I don't want anyone counting her out or thinking the worst. She can come back from this and live a healthy and happy life. As of right now though, she has slipped into a coma and she's also heavily sedated. The ventilator will be doing one hundred percent of the breathing for her and we're going to monitor her closely. Her vitals just stabilized for the first time since she came in, so things are already looking up. We're going to take this moment by moment and--" The doctor was interrupted by my dad walking back in. She stepped to the side to make room for him, and we asked her to repeat it for him and she did.

Dr. Oswald continued to tell us that Jax had a tube draining blood from her brain but not to be alarmed by it. Not to be alarmed by it? How the fuck were we not supposed to be alarmed by my sister having a part of her skull removed for swelling and bleeding on her fuckin' brain? I couldn't even wrap my mind around whatever else she was saying. I walked out dazed, confused, shook, and hurt to my core. I needed a drink and I needed it *now.*

"Zionna!" I turned around and Fresh was running towards me just as the elevator dinged. I stood there waiting for him and as soon as he reached me, he pulled me into his arms, and I completely lost it. I screamed, yelled, and cried into his chest. There was no fuckin' way I could live in this world without my damn sister. No fuckin' way possible.

Messiah

I listened as the doctor finished telling us about Jaxsyn and went straight into Sydnee's injuries. I didn't know who was worse off. The bones in Sydnee's legs were shattered, both of her arms were broken, her collar bone was fractured, her right wrist was cracked and so was three of her ribs which caused damage to her lungs. Like Jaxsyn, she wasn't breathing on her own yet. The only plus to Syd's condition was that surprisingly her spinal cord had no damage and she didn't have any serious neck or brain injuries. In my opinion, she was lucky as hell. Blessed, really. This bitch made nigga Gato dropped her little ass from a hovering fuckin' helicopter. Granted, he wasn't that high in the air but still. Who the fuck even does this kind of shit? By far this was the craziest muthafucka I ever encountered.

"When can I see Jaxsyn?" I asked the doctor. "Can her and our son be in the same room or when is he getting discharged? I need to be by her side but I'm not leaving my son either."

"We're just observing your son overnight. I'm sure we can make some adjustments for you to be with both of them. He'll be released in the morning. We're trying to place both women close to each other so it's more convenient. Give us about fifteen minutes and we'll send someone to get you." She gave us a tight-lipped kind smirk and walked away.

Giz bear hugged me, and I swear I needed that shit. I could only take so much, and it was times like this that my brother proved he had me, by simply lightening my load. Giz stepped into that role and I could never repay him for everything he's done for me over the last couple of years and especially recently. "We got you fam. On God, we do." He tapped my back before letting me go and I nodded. "They gon' be straight, Brian." Giz hugged him too. That man was going through it. Two daughters laid up in the hospital, one missing, the love of is his life barely hanging on, his sons hadn't said shit to him since he admitted to loving Kabrina more than their momma, plus her scandalous ass acts had to be weighing heavily on his mental too.

"I know." He looked at Junior and his eyes glazed over. "I umm, I'll be back." Brian walked out and we all shook our heads. It was hard not to feel bad for him.

It took two hours for these niggas to find rooms together and accommodate my son and Jax so we could all be in the same room. I end up having to come out of some bread just to force the staff to do their damn jobs. It was money well spent though and they put us in a private suite.

"Wow, she's gorgeous." Mauricio said as soon as he walked into Jax's room and laid eyes on her. It caused me to smirk because there was no denying her beauty even as she laid in her hospital bed swollen with tubes coming from everywhere.

"She's even more gorgeous with her eyes open. They hold a light that I've never seen in anyone before. I'm convinced that it's her heart that shines through." I stroked the side of her face. I couldn't believe this shit was happening to her.

"They say the eyes are the windows to our souls."

"Because of her, I believe it."

We both got quiet and a few moments later he went to sit down. I kissed Jax's cheeks and lips repeatedly as I prayed over her. She didn't deserve this shit and I hoped, wished, and prayed that her outcome would be as positive as I felt it would. She told me several times that God hadn't brought us this far to just leave us. I believed her then and this wasn't the time to doubt it. That was the only thing that kept me from going crazy. This couldn't be it for us. I couldn't accept that he wanted her back before we got our happily ever after.

"You have a beautiful family. Your son looks just like the both of you."

"Thanks."

"Listen I--"

"Now ain't the time. We'll chop it up when the time is right. I hated yo' ass for a long ass time thinking you was out there just not giving a fuck. Me and bro been through a lot of shit, but we made it through, and we were finally good. Now your shit came to our doorstep and he's no longer here. I'm trying to mentally sort through this bullshit. All I want right now, other than my family to be whole again, is your fuckin' brother, his son, and revenge. Everything else is on the back burner for now."

"Understood." He stood up. "Let's make that happen." He patted my back as he walked towards the door. "Take tonight to spend with your family and don't worry about anything but their conditions. My brother's days are numbered, and I have several men working on it. I'll let you finish him off, but he killed my son, and for that, he gotta see me." He walked out and I believed him.

****

Kabrina's health had gotten slightly better, and it was just enough to give us all a tiny glimmer of much needed hope. Although she was still weak and her condition had only gotten a little better, she made it past the forty-eight-hour mark and at this point, we had to take the baby steps as huge strides in the right direction. Between her, Jax, and Syd we yearned for a small victory and she was the one giving it to us. Unfortunately, neither Jaxsyn nor Sydnee had woken up and their prognosis hadn't

108

changed either. Their conditions didn't worsen though, which was a victory that we could all appreciate.

"Up, DaDa." Jeniah reached for me and I smiled. I still couldn't believe how big and smart my babies are. I picked her up and she wanted to see her mommy, so I leaned forward and let her kiss Jax again. Baby girl was super attached. They all are, but this lil one was on my ass about her momma. I didn't mind though. I had all three of my babies and that was nothing short of a blessing.

Jax and I had been through hell but so had they. I'm going to spend the rest of my life making this shit up to them. Especially my son. Seeing Junior protect Kabrina with that plastic sword, made me both proud that my son came into this world thorough, and hurt that he even had to experience that. I want better for him. My kids will never experience shit their parents went through. Jax and I are breaking cycles and showing our children something different. This shit ain't it and I felt guilty as fuck all over again.

"You look better today." Z walked in with Fresh, and I looked at both of them for a moment before I responded.

"Thank my lil ones for that." I focused my attention back on the kids as she walked over to Jax and started whispering something in her ear. She had been doing that everyday all day and then crying. Fresh walked over to her and consoled her. I didn't know how I felt about that shit. She'd just told me she kissed her ex-boyfriend the other day and regretted it, but now she was gettin' kind of close to my cousin. Nash's cousin. That shit was weird for me. I almost wanted to pop off, but it wasn't like they were doin' shit wrong, but at the same time, once she was my brother's girl, she was my brothers' girl and that made her automatically off limits. He was no longer here but the same rules should have applied.

"Aye, y'all together or some shit?" I had watched them long enough and I was over it.

"Huh?"

"What?"

They answered at the same time and gave themselves away. I stared at their silly lookin' asses and shook my head. "I can't rock with it, but I can't stop grown people from being grown, so it is what it is. I ain't trying to see that shit though. I got too much going on to be distracted by some shit that don't have shit to do with shit. Feel me?" I said as the girls twirled on my index fingers making themselves dizzy so they could fall out in my arms.

"Nah... It ain't like that cuz. You know I lost my girl a couple years back to some stupid ass street shit. We can just relate to each other." Fresh made a face as he shrugged his shoulders, clearly not giving a fuck how I felt, but just showing me respect because of Nash.

"I'm hip, but I see what's happening between y'all even if y'all don't. It ain't my business so it is what it is Fresh. Like I said though, I got other things to worry about so do y'all shit somewhere else." I shut the conversation down which made the room feel thick but a few minutes later the vibe was back to normal. Wasn't no beef, I just wasn't rockin' with that shit and that's what I meant. My loyalty is to my brother even in death. She's the mother of Nash seed regardless of us having Nevaeh or not, and now our blood cousin was trying to hit. Yeah... Nah, I wasn't feeling that in the least bit.

After I put the kids to sleep in Jaxsyn's room and called my cousins to stand guard, I bounced. I had shit to handle. There was no way in hell I was letting shit go just because I had my son back. My woman is laying in a hospital fighting for her life, my brother is gone, Sydnee might never walk or talk again, they stole millions in meds and money from me, Gato's hoe ass walked around my fuckin' crib dropping our babies, and then killed Tab. They were coming at us hard over Mauricio and that's why I started going at their asses with that same energy.

I pulled up to one the Knight's club houses and put the blunt I had been smoking out before stepping out of the car. I hadn't been spending much time here since I had been released, for obvious reasons, but also because it didn't feel the same without Nash. We started this shit together and everything in these club houses reminded me of him and the fact that I was in this shit alone now.

"How's Jax?" Solo asked as soon as I walked in and I hugged him. I could tell I had taken him by surprise, but I didn't give a fuck. It had been a rocky couple years for us and this was my nigga. I had a million things and people to worry about and he was never one and didn't deserve to be treated like one.

"Same." I responded and he nodded. "I'm ready."

"Bring order to the floor!" He yelled out and everyone turned around. Normally that would have silenced the room but when my brothers saw me, they all rushed me. Some of them hadn't laid eyes on me since before I turned myself in. The love was genuine, and I appreciated all their well wishes for Jax and Junior. Solo called order again and everyone halted.

"Man, it feels good to be back y'all. I want to start by saying I fucked up and I'm man enough to admit that shit. After losing Nash it really fucked me up and I started looking at everyone like they were a suspect. I doubted my brothers because of Rodney and Martez behavior plus a few other things that I can't get into right now, but I was wrong. Y'all niggas ride hard for me and y'all didn't deserve the cold shoulder that I gave y'all, especially you Solo. You been our brother before we even had this MC. You-"

"Ain't no apologies needed Prez. It's all love." He shook his head and I nodded.

"I have some shit to handle so I won't be fully back in the MC for a few weeks but I'm back and I appreciate y'all." I tapped my heart, and they did the same. Normally we would be in our meeting room and when we're done speaking, me and Nash would hit the table twice and they hit it twice to confirm we all had a clear understanding, but I needed this to be personal. I needed them to know my words were genuine and straight from my heart.

I kicked it for about twenty more minutes with my Knights and then I made my way all the way to the back where our warehouse is located. I had a package waiting for me that I couldn't wait to get to.

"Wake yo bitch ass up." I slapped the dog shit out of Jose Vargas, that nigga Rodney's father and Mauricio's other big brother. I had been wanting to get my hands on him since I found out that Rodney's bitch ass pretended and played roles to become a Knight, just to infiltrate my shit. I never doubted my team before him, and one incident changed how I looked at everybody. It was hard to tell the difference between friends and foes, so sadly, it became fuck'em all.

Play time has been over and everybody that ever thought they could play me was getting destroyed one by one.

"I said wake the fuck up." I slapped that nigga again and he groaned.

"Wh… Wha…" His head hung low enough for his chin to touch his chest as a string of slob dripped from his mouth. "What is this?"

"Dear brother, this is when the shit hits the fan." Mauricio made his way to where we were, and Jose's head popped up. It's funny how he suddenly got that boost of energy at the sound of Mauricio's voice. They stared at each other until it was awkward for everyone looking at them. Jose had spotted a ghost, and Mauricio was staring at a rat.

"Where have you been?" Jose's tone was laced with anger and you could obviously tell that the level of hate he had for Mauricio, was as deep-seated as it appeared.

"Living. No thanks to you though, right?" Mauricio pointed to the old iron chair in the corner and one of his goons brought it to him. He pulled it across the floor scraping it against the concrete until he was directly in front of his big brother. He took a seat and Giz looked over at me with nothing but amusement in his expression.

"You deserved everything that came your way."

Mauricio nodded his head slowly. "Son." He called out and we heard footsteps walking our way making us all look back. In walked a nigga that looked like a lighter version of me. The crazy thing about me having the same face as them, was that I'd always thought I looked a lot like the people on my mother's side of the family, but this shit right here was trippy.

He glanced my way and gave a head nod as he took his place next to his father. They both stared at Jose for a moment before Mauricio started again. I was ready to rush this shit along. I had left my family at the hospital to take care of this beef shit and I needed to get back.

"Two shots to the chest could have taken me away from him." He nodded towards his son. "You knew Destiny was pregnant with him and you didn't even hesitate to pull the trigger and step over what you thought was my dead body, like I wasn't *shit*." You could tell just by the way Mauricio moved and the way the words left his mouth that he was a very calculated man. He had been waiting patiently for this moment and when I finally told him this morning that we had Jose in our possession, he jumped at the chance to be here. I gave him the address and told him to meet us here at nine and his ass showed up an hour earlier. This was his moment, and I didn't intervene. He needed this and I understood completely. "Obviously you knew about my other sons too." He chuckled to himself as

113

he put his hand out towards his son. "Y'all took my first born from me and more than you shooting me, you're going to pay for that." Dude passed him a gun and he swiftly shot Jose in the chest. The shock that covered his face made this whole shit worth it. "It was a good idea to take my grandkids?" He shot him again.

"Ahhhh you know how Fernando is motherfucker! You know how he is! I didn't have a choice. Fuuuuck." His leg was barely hangin' on from that second shot to the kneecap and his chest was oozing.

"Fernando is going to get what's coming to him too, but we're talking about you right now *muthafucka*!" Mauricio kicked that nigga in the chest Sparta style and then stood over him and emptied the clip. He stared at his handy work for a moment before looking back at me. "He would never go against Fernando and give us any information. We need Smitty for that, which is Fernando's right-hand man and in-house flunky."

"Funny you should say that." Gizmo smirked and nodded for us to follow him. The fuckin' sun was up, and it didn't even seem like we were in the warehouse that long. I needed to get back to my family. Just as I was about to tell them that I was out, my phone rang.

"Hello." I answered for Shawn.

"Cuz, get back to the hospital. The cops just showed up and cuffed Jaxsyn. They saying she's wanted for the murder of Mariah Smith."

"What the fuck!" I said in sheer disbelief as everyone turned around and looked at me. "I have to get back to the hospital now. Some shit is going on with Jax." Everybody started hopping in cars and on their bikes, burning out of the parking lot. This shit just wouldn't stop…

Zionna

I stood in the doorway of Kabrina's hospital room watching my dad cater to her every need. Her body was in a weakened state and she was barely moving, but the way her eyes followed him as he fixed her pillows and damn near sparkled each time their eyes met, made me smile. In a million years, I wouldn't have ever imagined this. Their love story was filled with trials, tribulations, and true love. I really adored them.

"I love you, baby. I'm about to go check on Jaxsyn and the kids and then Sydnee since I slept in here last night. I'll be back a little later." He bent down and kissed her lips as she placed her frail hand on the side of his face. They shared a moment and then he pecked her forehead before turning around to face me. "Shit Zionna." He grabbed his chest and I smiled.

"Sorry. I just love y'all and got caught up in the moment," I said honestly as he made his way towards me. We held on to each other for a moment before he kissed my head and asked about how I was doing. I loved that we were here in this moment. This is what I've needed from a parent my whole life. Even in the midst of everything he had going on, he still checked in with me daily, and I honestly appreciate him so much for it.

We talked for a few minutes and I told him that Sydnee's blood pressure had spiked and she had a fever that they were getting concerned about. That poor girl was going to have a long ass road ahead of her. It seemed like everyday something new was going wrong with her. Granted, the crazy ass nigga Gato dropped her from a helicopter and no matter how fuckin' low he was flying, it was still a huge fall, and the proof is in her condition. My dad was definitely trying to hold it all together, but we all knew how hard this whole situation was for him. None of us left him alone for long periods of time because this kind of pressure on a person doesn't always make a diamond. Sometime this kind of pressure makes people act irrationally and make decisions that they later regret or can't come back from.

I stayed in Kabrina's room for about an hour since they finally agreed to letting me wash her hair. The hospital staff slacked on cleaning her hair properly. She still had matted patches of dried blood throughout her head, and I refused to let her go another day like that. If they were too lazy or busy to do what I asked them to do yesterday, I would handle it. Her body was battered from them beating her but not to the point that I couldn't help her with her hygiene and today I decided not to take no as an answer.

As a nurse I didn't play when it came to my patients, so I definitely wasn't about to play about my family. This was something I shouldn't have even had to check the staff about. When I hugged her and she was musty, I was pissed. I'm sure that smell was killing Kabrina slowly inside too. Having to smell and relive whatever she went through wasn't right and I raised hell and threw my experience around until one of the nurses begged to assist me with bathing her from head to toe. I washed her hair thoroughly and rubbed her down in cocoa butter lotion from my purse. She looked beautiful as usual, but her skin was pale and her eyes had dark circles around them. She didn't look like the old junky that she used to be, but she damn sure looked like she was on her way again. I knew with my dad by her side he wouldn't allow her to go down that road again, so I didn't even allow my mind to go there. She was in good hands.

After taking care of things with Kabrina, I made my way to Jaxsyn's room. I always made her, and the kids last since there was more to do in her room. Junior couldn't get around because of his leg and the girls have been so happy that their brother is back that they didn't give him any breaks or breathing room. All day its brother do this, brother do that, come here brother. Brother, brother, brother; and it never fails, he always ends up hurting his leg. Now we make him lay his lil butt down and they have to bring the toys to him so most of the time I'm watching them and keeping Jaxsyn company. I don't want her to think for one moment that I'm not beside her. I pray over her, reminisce with her, tell her about what the kids are doing all day, I let her know that Sih is okay, and I tell her about me and Fresh.

Fresh, I can't even say his name without smiling. He's such an amazing person. There's nothing sexual between us or anything like that because at the end of the day, he's still Nash and Sih's cousin, but I've honestly never felt more understood by someone the way I feel understood by him. Granny Knight raised him, so he did get a break from life around fourteen years old but before then, both of his parents were on drugs and his momma used to let her home girls have sex with him when they got drunk. He said they would have parties and his momma's friends would comment on how handsome he was, and she would be like *gone in there and get the dick, it's big already.* He told me how he lost his virginity to his God mother when he was eleven and she didn't stop creeping into his room until he was thirteen. The only reason she stopped is because their house caught on fire, his momma fell asleep cooking. That's when he moved with Granny Knight the first time and caught a break.

He could relate to having to fend for yourself at an early age and more than anything else, he could relate to the darkness I slipped into after Nash died. His girl was killed in a shoot-out a couple years ago and he can barely talk about her without getting choked up. She was pregnant at the time too, so he lost her and the baby over some beef

117

that wasn't even his own just like with Nash. He started drinking like me but instead of running away from the people he loved like I did, he turned to them and they held him down and made sure he bounced back. That's what he provides for me. The security and confidence to bounce back. There's not a day that goes by that I don't still mourn Nash and want to pick up a drink to numb my pain, and most of the time I do.

The first night Fresh and I chopped it up it was an all-nighter. I told him everything including me giving up my baby, regretting it, and then accepting my decision. I told him about running to Arizona and continuing my destructive behavior there in private. He told me about being so drunk he woke up on the side of the road, drenched in his own piss, with a blunt stuck to his dried lips, hanging halfway out of the car, as other cars drove by. He couldn't remember where he was coming from or headed to since he was nowhere near his house or anyone that he knew. We just clicked, because I had more nights like that than I cared to admit out loud, but it felt so good that I wasn't alone, and someone knew what I felt from experience.

"Name?"

"Excuse me?" I looked at this big nigga guarding my sister's door like he was crazy, as he eyed two police officers standing off to the side looking red in the face and pissed off.

"Who are you?" I asked.

"Name?"

"Zionna."

"Go ahead." He gave a subtle nod towards the door and I stared at him for a moment before reaching for the handle. I walked in and Messiah was going the fuck off on whoever he was on the phone with. That wasn't rare, especially these days, but all of this was going down with the kids in the room. This had to be serious because he has never really turned up like this in front of them and it made my stomach flutter with uncertainty. No two days in our lives were the same these days so I was nervous to even find out what caused him to act this way as everyone just watched.

"Fuck that bitch! She didn't give a fuck about my brother outside of what he could do for her and the dick he dropped in her. They better hide that bitch under the biggest fuckin' rock they can find or in the deepest cave because when my people find that hoe, it's over." He hung up and everyone was still staring at him. He shot Giz a look and with no words spoken, Giz, Shawn, and Fresh stood to their feet and started making their way out of the room.

"You good?" Fresh asked before he walked out, and I smiled.

"Yeah."

"Bet." His height allowed him to kiss the top of my head and then walk out with his cousins. I turned and Messiah looked disgusted with me.

"It's really nothing going on Sih," I said and he didn't say shit back. We were just good and now he was in his feelings. "Who is the guy at the door?"

"My... Mauricio's people. Toya told the police that Jaxsyn killed Mariah and they came and cuffed her with no fuckin' proof. I went stupid in this bitch. Mauricio pulled some strings to get the police to fall back and put one of his men on the door to make sure no one bothered her again." He shook his head and stared lovingly at Jaxsyn. "They had my baby cuffed and she's in a coma fighting for her fuckin' life. Niggas really trying me." He leaned forward and kissed her lips as he whispered something to her. Their love was deep and beautiful, and I loved being a witness to something so great. It gave me hope that I would someday have that again.

"DaDa." Jeniah patted his leg. "Up." She reached and without a second thought he picked her up so she could kiss Jaxsyn. This was what she did everyday all day. She would lay on Jax for hours playing on my phone not saying a word. Eventually her brother and sister would join her and fall asleep on their mother. It was the saddest most beautiful thing you'd ever want to see.

Messiah made call after call after call as I played with the kids. Everyone was feeling his wrath, and no one wanted to get in his way. He was stuck between pulling kick doors like his boo and staying by her side. That was causing him to be even more pissed and irritated. The staff was coming and going without saying one word to him. Normally these thirsty ass hoes would be all in his face, seconds from dropping to their knees but today they steered clear, and it was definitely in their best interest to do so. One thing you don't do, is mess with this man's family. That's when you get a completely different version of him.

"Aye, I gotta make a run. Don't leave." He barked at me and walked over to Jaxsyn. "I love you, Tink. I'm stepping out for a little while, but you know daddy will be right back. I'm leaving Z in here with the kids and we have guards at the door. Relax and I'll see you in a minute." He double pecked her lips and kissed the kids before he walked out. This whole Fresh situation really had him treating me like shit, but it honestly wasn't anything between us to have him acting like that towards me. I wouldn't necessarily say I didn't like how Fresh made me feel when we're around each other, but in no way shape or form would I disrespect Nash's memory and it hurt that Messiah treated me like he didn't know that.

Messiah

I was on a straight up warpath. I was chilling at the hospital with my family during the day and killing muthafuckas in cold blood at night. I sent Jose's head to his wife with five of Smitty's fingers in his mouth. Smitty is Fernando's right-hand man so I made sure to leave his pinky ring on his finger, so they knew exactly what time it was. There was no mistaking where I was ready to go with Fernando and Gato. A day later one of my techs told me Jose's wife called a burner phone and talked for seven minutes. Once I knew she delivered the message, I ended that bitch and started picking off niggas in the Vargas Cartel like I was playing the Duck Hunt video game from back in the day. They weren't the only ones I was going after either. The muthafuckin' gloves were off and the longer my Tink was in a coma the harder I went. I handled both of Toya's parents and had her granny tied up with Rebecca and Smitty. I didn't give a damn who I had to take the fuck out from the goldfish to the granny. No one was exempt and I didn't feel an inkling of remorse.

"Hi Mommy," Jeniah said, and I smiled. She was... wait... shit! I hopped up quick as fuck and tripped over a toy almost stepping on Z who was on the floor playing a game with Junior. She screamed and looked at me like I was crazy.

"She's awake!" I grabbed Jax hand, and she looked confused. "I know baby. We'll explain everything to you."

"Sissy." Zionna started crying and Jax snatched her hand away from me and looked at Z. We both stared at each other and then her. I ran to the door and started calling for the doctors. I didn't know what the fuck that was about, but they asses better fuckin' fix it.

We had to clear all three kids out of the room and allow the staff to do their thing. I didn't want to be asked any questions about what had just happened so once I had security in the lobby and knew the kids were alright with Brian and Zionna, I walked off. My baby looked me in my face and snatched her hand away. Did she blame me for what happened to her? I swear a nigga can't win for losing.

The wait to go back into the room wasn't long at all. By the time I walked back up the nurse was walking up too, telling us we could go back inside. We all damn near sprinted to her room. She had less bandages on her head, the tube that was down her throat was gone and most of the other tubes she was connected to was gone as well. She still had the drainage bag for her catheter connected, and the feeding tube, other than that, she had an IV.

"Baby." Brian ran to her and tears rolled down her face. Once again, Zionna and I looked at each other.

"He… He…" Brian let her go and we all stared at her. She couldn't get her words out.

"He who Jax? Junior?" Zionna asked and looked at our son that she was holding but Jax just stared at him like she was puzzled. No fuckin' way! She didn't even know her son that she's spent every day searching for and crying over. Why the fuck couldn't my baby talk to us? I needed answers and they better come quick with them before I go ham in this bitch. "What is this honey?" Z held up one of the oranges she was about to peel for the kids.

"Ap… Aaaap…"

"It's okay Boo. Apple?" Zionna asked and Jax nodded. I snatched the door open so hard I'm surprised it didn't fly off the fuckin' hinges. "Get her muthfuckin' doctor right now," I said through gritted teeth. I was pissed the fuck off. How can his raggedy ass go in her room and not notice that something didn't seem right... Normally the medical staff explains the patient's condition to them, but they just said fuck Jax and I wasn't having it. When she didn't respond or kept looking confused, nothing went off in this so-called medical professional's head. I was fuckin' pissed because I stay on their ass about doing their jobs and this was another example of their bullshit.

"Hey." I heard come from behind me and it was Mauricio. For the last couple weeks, he had been by my side in the street and right here in the hospital with me, pulling long ass nights and early mornings for both. The kids had grown to love him, and Nevaeh even calls him "grampy" or paw paw, which he loves. I allowed it because the nigga is her grandfather and I can't lie, he's great with them. Jeniah's spoiled ass could be standoffish sometimes, but that's just my baby and how she'll play you.

"Hey. They called you?"

"No. Just coming to check on everyone. Something going on?"

I nodded. "She's up." His excitement matched ours as if he knew her and I thought that was dope. The moment didn't last long when I told him everything. He immediately walked away and started making calls. I didn't know what he was trying to do but judging by his behavior over the last few weeks, he's about action and I fuck with that heavy. If he could do anything for her, I was accepting it. I can't gamble with my baby's life or allow my ego to block what could be a blessing.

As soon as the doctor walked up, I slapped fire from his bitch ass and the world around us stood still. "Get yo' monkey ass in that fuckin' room and tell me what the fuck is wrong with my wife before you're next to get admitted. Had you not been rushing, you probably could have done your job right the first fuckin' time you were in there. You just weren't gon' say shit to her or explain to her what happened? Y'all better stop fuckin' playin' with me and mine." I muffed his bitch ass and stared him down.

"Mr. Kn--"

"Get. In. That. Fuckin'. Room." I pointed and followed behind him once he started walking. I looked at my dad's security and they were already doing damage control. I appreciated it but at the same time I didn't give a fuck about the consequences. The whole staff had me all the way out of my character, but on everything I love, they better stop testing me.

I stood back and watched closely as they ran test after test on my baby and asked her a million questions that she struggled to answer. She knew my name, but she couldn't remember who I was. The only people she was clear on is Zionna, Brian, and her brother Dawson, the rest of us, she just stared at like she was trying to figure it out. My chest was tight. If I hadn't hit that fuckin' pole we wouldn't even be in this predicament. Maybe I was to blame.

"Don't do that." Zionna walked over to me as I stared out of the window. The doctors said brain injuries can cause major damage, but they had been running test on Jaxsyn this whole time. According to the results, there was no drastic damage. The swelling had gone down and the tube that drained the blood from around her brain had been removed from her head. Everyone kept saying all this shit was great signs and then she wakes up and don't know her own children. The doctor said she was just confused which was normal and she may have to learn a few things all over again, but it wasn't amnesia which gave us hope. They kept telling us not to worry but how could I not worry though? That was like asking water not to get shit wet.

"Do what?"

"Blame yourself?"

"Who else am I supposed to blame Zionna? I ran us into a fuckin' pole."

"Because a lunatic was shooting at you from a damn helicopter Sih! He dropped our sister in front of you while you were speeding to get away from him. What were you supposed to do? You did what you thought was best and she's alive because of it. If you didn't swerve and you'd hit Syd, you would have killed her instantly and who's to say he wouldn't have kept shooting and killed all three of y'all? Count your blessings bro and don't do this to yourself. This ain't your fault in the least bit." She walked away and the one thing that stood out to me the most was me counting my blessings. I looked over at Jaxsyn and she was quietly watching Nevaeh and Junior play at the end of her bed as Jeniah laid on her with someone's phone like they did every day. We were undoubtedly in the midst of a storm, but we were blessed. A month ago, I was scared my baby was going to get committed into a mental institution because two of our kids were missing and here we were, all together in one room.

"Can y'all give us some time?" I looked around the room at everyone and they all nodded. I had everyone shook but at the same time they understood how heavy this shit was. Mauricio stopped on his way out and told me that he had specialists ready to step in and they could do it all from our home. I told him I needed to get us out of that house. I quickly explained how Gato was all through our home and that's where all this shit started, or so I thought. Our home was no longer a sanctuary for Jax but a reminder of our darkest and most trying times. As a man, I couldn't bring my woman back into that environment, my children either.

Mauricio was furious about the details that I hadn't shared before now. That was just more fuel to the fire, and I could hear it in his tone. He never showed his hand, so his expression never changed. He told me not to worry about anything other than the four people behind me and that he would take care of everything. I didn't know what he meant, and he walked away before I could object or gain clarity. It was clear that my temper came directly from him.

"DaDa can mommy play?" Junior asked and I smiled.

"Not yet big boy but she will soon." I kissed his head and pulled a chair on the side of the bed.

"He... He." I could see Jaxsyn was frustrated as she attempted to speak again. She had been saying this all day and we couldn't figure out what she was trying to tell us. She couldn't even write it because it was gibberish. She thought she was writing to us, but it was all squiggly lines. That was definitely Zionna's breaking point, she ran out of the room crying hysterically and of course Fresh went to help her. Jaxsyn was confused about everything and it was hard to experience, but we knew it was harder for her.

"You'll be able to tell us soon baby. I promise." We stared at each other before she said okay. "Until that happens, let's start over. Okay?" I stood and picked Jeniah up with her little clingy ass. She giggled and I climbed in bed with them. I brought Jax into my arms, and the kids laid on us. It was their bedtime anyway, so this was perfect. "So I'm standing in the parking lot with my Knights, that's my motorcycle club," She looked surprised and I chuckled. "Aye, don't look like that, ya man is that nigga out here." She smiled and she had no idea how long I'd waited to see that. I stared at her for a moment just taking in her perfection, before I continued. "Anyway, you and Zionna pull up and step out of your Range Rover. I like to believe it was love at first sight when I laid eyes on you." She looked up at me and I nodded my head. "Really! When you came out of the store, my prospects surrounded your truck and blocked you in. I couldn't let you get away. I had to have you and I got you." She snuggled into my embrace as I told her all about our life together. The good, the bad, and the ugly. With every word I spoke, I could actually feel myself falling deeper in love with her. When I made it to the moment we were in now, Jax was in tears. She took my face into her hands and kissed me passionately, causing tears to roll down my face. This was my first time breathing with ease in weeks. With Jax's life hanging in the balance, I've been fucked up. Every second of everyday I was begging her to come back to me and our children. Having her in my arms felt surreal and I leaned in, deepening our kiss, and breathing her in. I missed my Tink so much. For the rest of the night, I held her closely and continued to tell her stories about our children and us, as we kissed and escaped into our own world like we've always done. Jax has always had a fire burning inside of her that would never allow her to give up on anything, and I saw it blazing in her eyes as I held her. We were going to be good, and I knew it without a shadow of doubt.

Rebecca

Smitty had been gone for days and the silence seemed so loud. My thoughts were haunting me and so was my guilt. Karma wasn't just affecting me in the physical form but also mentally. I had peed on myself twelve times so far and my stomach was growling, rumbling, and doing summersaults. It was trying to get rid of its last bit of waste because lord knows I hadn't eaten anything since I've been wherever I am. I had no clue as to where I was or what was going to happen. I had been blindfolded since the day we were snatched out of the house and literally thrown into the back of some van. There was no way of me even knowing how much time had passed.

When they threw us in the back of the van, I slammed my head against something metal and damn near passed out. Before I could catch my bearings, Smitty landed directly on top of me with all of his body weight directly on my chest. There were tools everywhere and it was no space to move. Blood was definitely pouring from my head, but my wrist was bound together behind me digging into my back with Smitty's weight making it worse. We rode like that for what seemed like hours and I struggled to breathe the whole time. A few times I thought I wasn't going to make it and I was fine with that.

How stupid was I to think Messiah would just pick up his son and carry on with his life? I knew they would never speak to me or want me around, but they came in that damn house like gang busters, and I just knew I was dead. Hell, at this point I wish I would have had a heart attack that day when they came busting into the house and ended it all right there. I have no idea what these people are going to do with me. What I do know is that Smitty was taken away and he never came back, and I feared that I was next.

Day and night I thought about my children and how much more of me they deserved. I've been jealous of their bond with Brian for years, but in reality, I knew why. I made things look pretty on the outside while Brian made sure they were loved and appreciated on the inside. We looked picture perfect to the world, so I felt like my home was doing well. That gave me time to focus on my other family that was filled with pain. Ollie and Dominic were broken over their mother and needed me. I neglected the children I gave birth to for them. That makes me a shitty fuckin' parent and no better than my own. It actually makes me worse if I'm completely honest. My family are horrible racist people but that's their reason for disowning me. I made a decision that they hated. My children were perfect and still couldn't have more than basic access to me on the daily, and a sliver of my time on most holidays. I treated my own like shit and this quiet time had my thoughts replaying their faces when I said mommy had to work as Brian looked on, not believing a word I was saying and not giving enough fucks to address it. Funny where your mind goes when you're staring death in the face.

One bad decision after another lead me here and none of it was worth it in the end. I couldn't honestly sit in this chair and say fuck what happens next, at least I lived a good life. That would be a lie. All that plotting and arguing with Brian over the years, and his love for Kabrina still never wavered. He still wouldn't give up on her no matter how low her habit dragged her down. Every single time she fell, he was right there picking her up and reminding her to get herself together for Jax. No matter how much shit I did for Fernando and the boys, it was never enough either. Even after betraying my own blood, Fernando disrespected me and treated me like I wasn't shit to him. Dominic told me not to even call him by his name anymore. He and I share something that I don't even share with his father and that's how he chose to treat me over a mistake.

Lord, if I could only go back and do everything over. There is no doubt in my mind that I would go all the way back to the beginning, and abort Dawson before telling my family or Brian. That sounds so fucked up, but I would have continued living my life drama free. Unfortunately, there is no do overs in life, and this is where the decisions I've made landed me; in an undisclosed location, beaten, hungry, cold, and alone. Well… not alone. I could faintly hear someone crying in the distance and I guess that person's fate matched mine.

My head swiveled around as I heard footsteps coming towards me. This was the same thing we heard before Smitty was taken away. I pretended to be asleep that time, but they were here and gone so quick it didn't even matter. They came specifically for him and didn't even acknowledge my presence.

I squinted my eyes like a vampire that had just been exposed to the sun as soon as my blindfold was snatched off. The person said nothing as my eyes adjusted. Once I was focused, my bladder released again. Messiah's face scrunched up as him and all the men with him watched pee roll off of the chair I was sitting in.

"Oh you scared, scared huh?" One of the men said and they all shook their heads in pure disgust. They all looked exactly alike but the man to Messiah's right was undoubtedly Mauricio. I had seen hundreds of pictures of him in the family library. The Vargas Estate is not just Fernando's home but the family estate and no matter how mad he got, he never destroyed any memories that included Mauricio.

"Are those hunger pains digging in yet? Yeah, that's how Jax felt as a child when you were feeding her mother drugs. You scared, alone, feel deserted? So did my baby when you plotted against her parents." His tone was so harsh, it made me quiver. "I decided since I was already here, I would come inform you on what's happening in the real world. Your stepson Gato kidnapped Alyssa who is pregnant with a married man's baby. He made sure we knew that he took her because you let us get Junior. Once again, he was a step ahead so as we left the house with Junior and Kabrina, Gato hovered over us in a fuckin' helicopter shooting into the car I was driving. The car that had my son inside, the grandson you claimed to love. Then out of nowhere he dropped Sydnee from that helicopter as I was doing well over a hundred miles per hour trying to escape him.

"I swerved to avoid hitting her and sent Jaxsyn and Junior headfirst through the windshield when I hit a light pole. Jax brain was swollen, and they had to cut her skull to drain the blood. Sydnee was only captured by him because she left our home and went looking for you. It was hard for her to grasp your betrayal. She assumed there had to be a better explanation for your actions other than pure jealousy. She died from internal bleeding this morning. The fall was too much for her little body." He nodded and the blindfold was put back on. I didn't even know someone was behind me and I flinched at how rough he was. The steps started to fade and moments later those faint sounds I heard in the distance were now blood curdling screams and then just like with Smitty, things all of a sudden went eerily silent and once again, I was alone with my thoughts. My baby girl was dead... My heart broke and I yelped out in agony from a pain that I didn't even know existed. My babies. I couldn't even wrap my mind around the bomb that was just dropped on me. They all deserved better than what I've gotten them involved in and her murder was on my hands, but also on her father's hands...

Zionna

Brian was literally a zombie. Everyone in our circle was worried sick about him, and Kabrina wouldn't let him leave her bed. He had been in her room for almost two days straight, crying in her arms. He was no good to anyone and I couldn't even imagine the level of pain he was enduring. Granted, Syd was getting progressively worse over the last few days. She kept having seizures back-to-back and they couldn't figure out why. Her fevers would spike out of nowhere too, but we never thought we would get called into her room in the wee hours of the morning telling us that she was already gone. That pain hit different. We were just on vacation bonding and building, now she was gone. *Over what?* That's what I keep asking myself. What the fuck is this over? A jealous ass nigga with daddy issues? Fernando is a grown ass man and to say Rebecca had been around him all these years, she should have put her expertise to good use because his stupid ass needed a session. His hate for Mauricio is a sick obsession and has left a trail of dead and battered bodies. Including his own son.

We chose not to tell Jaxsyn about Sydnee. We may have been wrong to make that call but the work that we were putting into bringing Jax back to us was a constant everyday thing. Messiah turned everything into a lesson when it came to her so she could become more familiar with basic things like fruit and everyday items. He had the kids playing with her and he made it fun for all four of them. If there was ever a man that one hundred percent deserved my sister, it's Messiah fuckin' Knight. Wow... For weeks he's poured himself into my sister and has been present for her a thousand percent. She was doing so much better too. Even though her speech was taking the longest to come around, he was working diligently to help her improve everything else that was within his reach. It felt damn good to walk into her room and see her smiling from ear to ear at him acting a damn fool just to put a smile on her face, as she battled through the most trying time of her life.

"Nash." Mine and Messiah's head snapped around and looked at Jaxsyn. She was staring in our direction and she repeated herself. We were putting the kids to sleep and we both stopped and walked over to her. "He... He's..." She closed her eyes and tried to relax. Now that she was coming around, she gets really frustrated when she can't understand something or when she can't express herself the way she wants to. That's why Messiah tries to keep the lessons lightweight and fun. We didn't want her doing too much, too soon.

"Just breathe baby. Remember? Deep breaths." Messiah kissed her forehead and stroked her hand. She took a deep breath as instructed and when she opened her eyes they were filled with tears and landed on me.

"He's... not... mad... at... you." Her words came out barely audible, but we could understand her, and I covered my mouth as the water works silently started. "Tighten... up. Drinks...no more." I was a ball of emotions. "Fresh is... good... hands..." I backed away from the bed and stumbled on Junior's truck. Messiah grabbed my arm before I fell backwards, and I broke the fuck down. I was a wreck and she looked up at Sih.

"No more blaming. He... so... proud. Said Ne... Ne..." She took another breath as her nostrils flared but she regained her composure. "Nevaeh... looks... like... Nana." Messiah gasped and his grip on me tightened. I could feel him shaking but his face remained calm.

"When did he say that baby?"

"We... spent... everrrrry... every day to-geth-er."

Messiah kissed her head repeatedly.

"I remember now." We both stared at her as she slowly pointed out things in the room that she had been struggling to remember or was just flat out confused about. In the wake of Sydnee's passing, this was a really good pick me up. Honestly, the family needed this. We tested her writing skills but that still needed some work. She knew how to spell but that still wasn't translating to paper. She still had a long road ahead of her, but we were positive that her outcome would be great, especially after the progress she had made.

Before leaving the hospital, I went to visit Brian and Kabrina again. He was asleep and she was stroking his head.

"He's been sleep for about an hour." She was still in a weakened state but doing much better. The color was back in her face and she had put on a couple pounds. The doctors said she can go into rehab next week and she was looking forward to it. She said she wanted her old clean life back, and I understood that more than she realized.

"He needs the rest."

She looked down at him and nodded her head. "How's my baby?"

"Good." I smiled. "She's talking more and we're starting to see a lot more of the old Jaxsyn coming through. Her road is going to be long and bumpy, but you know we got her. Messiah and his dad are working overtime to make sure she gets the very best care, so she'll be a-okay."

She smirked. "She's a fighter. Stronger than I could ever be."

"You and me both." I agreed and we kicked it for about an hour before I let her know that I was leaving. Brian was still sleeping, and I needed to head home.

"Hey." I smiled at Fresh as I walked out of Kabrina's room.

"Hey. My cousin said you was probably down here." He pushed himself off the wall he was leaning against and hugged me. I inhaled his cologne and then let him go.

"Yeah. I need a mental break so I'm leaving for the day. Sih will call me if he needs me to come back."

"Come on, let me feed you. He said y'all ain't ate shit all day. I just texted Shawn and told him to bring Sih some food. Y'all be around this bitch starving with a million niggas on payroll."

I smiled again. "Some days food doesn't even cross our minds, well, at least not mine."

"Understandable." He hit the button to the elevator and Jaxsyn's words ran through my mind. No, Fresh and I still hadn't done anything or even attempted to. We don't even flirt but to say I wasn't attracted to him would be me lying. He's a sexy ass chocolate man that stands a good 6' 2" with one of the sexiest builds I've ever laid eyes on. Tattoos covered his neck and more than once I wanted to explore how far they go down, but I quickly readjust my thoughts. Hearing Jaxsyn tell me that Nash said I was in good hands with Fresh made me feel like no matter how this may look to Messiah and the rest of the world, it may be something to explore. I had way too much on my plate right now, but I could see us crossing the line in the future. My only concern was disappointing Nash, and Jax words gave me the assurance I needed.

Alyssa

I was positive that if my baby wasn't already dead, then it would be soon. I didn't know how long I was in the room I was being held in, but it had to have been days. There were no windows but even with the sleepiness from being pregnant I could tell the difference between when I was taking a nap and when my body was telling me it's "bedtime." That's when I would know I was about to go into another day.

That first day that I was forced into the trunk I woke up beaten, bloody, and bruised. I hadn't even remembered the guy putting his hands on me but the soreness, plus the black and purple marks all over my body were a dead giveaway. I hadn't seen or heard anyone since then. No food, no water, no contact. I was going crazy, but I also knew that if someone was to come in here, that meant I was dead, so I had no complaints. Leave me in this room until Messiah finds me because if I know anything about my brother, he was looking and looking hard. He knew I had nothing to do with what Sandy and my mother had going on which is why he trusted me in the car with Jax and my niece. He was going to find me, I just hoped it was in time.

I rubbed my stomach and laid on the hard concrete floor. The room I was held in was painted all white, but it was completely concrete from the ceiling to the floor. There was no comfortable position, so I just had to adjust and deal. I dozed off and woke up to something crawling on my hand. My eyes were still closed so I just flicked it off, but I felt it again. Slowly my lids became ajar, and I lost my mind. The floor was covered with spiders of all sizes. I started screaming and trying to knock them off of me. The room filled with laughs at my expense, but no one was in there with me which meant they had been watching me. I could feel someone watching me but in an all-white room I expected to see a black device or red dot indicating I was being watched, there was literally nothing. Now I know I just couldn't see it, but his sick ass had been close the whole time, while watching my baby slowly dying inside of me. Sick.

I spent what had to be hours killing all those spiders, leaving only a small space where guts didn't pave the floor. I ended up having to take my shirt off to shoo them away from where I slept so I wouldn't kill them all over the floor and then have nowhere to lay. I was tired and the little bit of energy that I did have, had been depleted. I laid back down, but I was terrified to close my eyes again not knowing what he would do to me next. Eventually my sleepiness took over and I was out like a light.

When I woke up, I thought I was losing my mind once again. The room was no longer white it was now green, the dead spiders had been cleaned up, and I had a small unopened bottle of water next to me and one White Castle burger. I squeezed the bottle just in case they punctured it with a small hole and once nothing came out, I drank the whole thing in one gulp. I'm sure they did something to the burger, but I checked it anyway. I didn't see anything but obviously he liked playing games and since we've come this far, it was obviously chess and not checkers. I ate the burger and licked my fingers. My stomach growled at that teaser and tears filled my eyes to the brim. I was failing my baby already and I couldn't help blaming my mother for the predicament I found myself in. She brought these people into my world and now I was going to die because of it. My baby was going to die because of it. How could I ever look at her the same? How could any of us? Or maybe this tied into my karma for sleeping with a married man… Something I knew I shouldn't have done.

The door unlocked interrupting my thoughts and I started shaking uncontrollably. A girl came running in before I could even embrace the death that I just knew was coming my way.

"Hurry up and eat this and take these. He's not watching right now so hurry up. Give me that bottle, here's a new one and hurry up and drink this one. I downed the new bottle of water as she passed me a fresh one and I gave her the empty one I'd finished earlier. She was literally shoving burgers into my mouth and I was swallowing as quickly as I could. "I may not be able to do this again but that's a week of prenatal vitamins so sip that water slow. Whatever you do, act distraught and beat down by his games. He loves seeing people weak and broken." Just as quickly as she came, she was gone. I had no idea who she was, how she knew I was here, or how she knew I was pregnant, but I was thankful. I cried for the rest of the night because I was grateful, but I also knew that death was still looming over me and it was just a matter of time. This man was a monster and the sheer terror in that girl's eyes and the way her hand was shaking as she tried to help me, confirmed what I already knew.

Please Messiah, save me.

Messiah

Surprisingly, Smitty's ass ain't as loyal as we assumed he would be, and my father was spot on when he said this is who we needed. I didn't take the same approach with him as I did with all the others that's found themselves in his predicament. This was a prideful Cuban man that's been in the Vargas Cartel for well over thirty years. He's seen it all and done it all. Hell, I took five of his fingers and he grunted the whole time but refused to show any more emotion than that.

I sat down in front of him with Mauricio and got right down to it. I put a needle in front of him at the table we were sitting at and then I laid out my tools. He knew he had two choices off rip, quick or painful, he was dying either way, but it was up to him how he went. "I'm not about to bullshit with you or play games. I don't have that type of time and I'm growing tired of the fuckin' games being played.

I need to end this shit and I need to end this shit quickly. I'm being dragged into some bullshit I had no idea about. I just met him a few weeks ago." I nodded towards Mauricio and I could tell Smitty was surprised so I continued, "Whatever that crazy muthafucka is over there thinking, he's wrong. My brother and I built our name off of grinding. We busted our asses and hated this nigga every second of the way because we thought he knew about us and bounced, but he didn't. Your people are doing all this shit for absolutely nothing." His thoughts were running wild, and he stared me in the eyes searching for a lie. He wasn't going to find one, so I let him do his thing. "Tell me what I need to know to end this shit."

"You know me Smitty." Mauricio spoke up. "I would have never left my children to handle this life alone, and you know damn well I had no ill will towards Fernando. Pop didn't ask me to step down because Fernando had a tantrum, like everyone assumed. I'm the one that brought the idea to Pop and begged him to reconsider. I didn't need that life like Fernando did so after a couple weeks Pop finally gave in and made the changes. I knew I could make money blindfolded with my hands tied behind my back. I didn't need the Cartel or a title, it didn't make a difference to me. This beef is senseless and one sided."

"Fernando wants to be the best, and when you're aware that you aren't the best, well, then you have to beat the best, right? You embarrassed Fernando one too many times and caused this rift between the two of yous." Smitty finally spoke. "You were always the star Mauricio. Of all the children in the Vargas family, the last one was the one to steal Antonio's heart right along with everyone else's. You were just like Antonio from the moment you entered this world and he loved it. You looked like him, walked, talked, and acted, just like your father. He had you all the time and the rest of the kids both his own children, as well as his nieces and nephews, became jealous. Your brothers used to beg for his attention through their wild behavior, but his attention gravitated to you naturally and effortlessly.

Fernando took Antonio's interest in you the hardest because he's the oldest and had been vying for his father's attention the longest. Nothing he ever did was good enough, so it was no surprise to anyone that Antonio chose to pass the business to you. On top of the fact that everything you touched in those streets turned to gold. You were the obvious choice either way, but Fernando couldn't stop his jealousy from rearing its ugly head. When you stepped down and he took your place, he turned into more of an asshole than he had ever been." He chuckled to himself and shook his head as if he was thinking back to that time.

"That's until the business started to slow up and people that we had been dealing with for a lifetime, stopped coming around. That was happening for months before we found out that you started doing your own thing and people were leaving us to go with you. Fernando snapped. Completely fuckin' lost his shit and turned into someone none of recognized. It became his personal mission to find and kill you. He found it disrespectful for you to not only flourish but also do so with the people that left him high and dry.

When Jose found you at that restaurant and shot you, they had been planning that for weeks. Fernando couldn't sleep if you were alive and made that clear several times a day. The estate was a mad house. Everyday our team was growing smaller and smaller because he was eliminating people for simply coming back with no information on you. Every man that worked for him was combing the streets searching for you. We celebrated the day Jose confirmed that he shot you. Everyone's life was hanging in the balance during that time and finally, men could breathe again.

The only flaw in Fernando's plan was him not knowing whether you died or not from the gunshot wound Jose assured him you received. When the cleanup crew arrived, you were gone. We searched for years and years, but everyone knew you were still making moves. The people that stopped doing business with us never came back, and they're all creatures of habit. Had they not been buying from you they, would have come back to us. We just had no solid proof since no one could find you to confirm it.

Somehow Fernando found out about Nashon and Messiah and they were driving flashy cars, bikes, and buying up property by the boat load. That was all the

141

conformation he needed that they were working for you, and to get to you, he had to go through them. After Ollie was killed that was where he lost me. Ollie didn't want this life and he was a damn good kid." He got emotional, but I didn't give a fuck about Ollie or no other nigga that came at me and my family whether they wanted to or not. Nash lost his life over their bullshit and I had zero sympathy.

"Where is Gato?" Ignoring the moment he was having, I continued with my questions.

"He's a live wire and could be a number of places. Get me a pen."

Mauricio called one of his men and they gave Smitty a pen and a small notepad. He wrote down several addresses and informed us that Fernando still lives at the Vargas Estate up North. He said Fernando had no confirmed plans to come after us once he found out we captured his men. He figured they might talk and put an end to everything they had in place. His men hadn't said shit, but it was good to know that these Vargas hoes had to switch shit up. Hopefully one of the addresses Smitty was writing down lead us to Alyssa. Not knowing where they had her was killing me.

Mauricio stood from the table and grabbed the needle, so I grabbed the paper and nodded towards Smitty giving him a nonverbal thanks and he returned the gesture. I turned around to walk out and Mauricio started to talk.

"I made no promises to you Smitty. I've never been one to beat around any bushes or bullshit anyone. You played a role in my first-born son dying, and for that, it's no painless revenge." I turned around just as he started beating Smitty with a hammer from my tool case. Each swing connected, and the sound bounced off the walls. Mauricio was fuckin' that old ass man up but I couldn't say I blamed him. Not only was this aggression from years of their senseless bullshit, but they were definitely responsible for Nash's untimely demise. He went in on Smitty as I stood and watched him release his wrath. After he was done, he stuck the needle in Smitty, and I chuckled to myself.

"I think he was already gone."

"He deserved to die twice." His tone was relaxed as he walked over to the sink and washed his hands. "You may not be ready to talk, but I am. I need you to understand that even though I just found out about you and Nashon, I love both of you unconditionally already. You're my flesh, my blood, my namesakes. Carmine is my world and now so are you, and my grandchildren. My heart mourns Nashon as if I've had him his whole life. As his father I feel like a failure and his passing will haunt me until I take my last breath. I'm huge on family son, and never in a million fucking years would I have ever abandoned you and your brother. Ever. I don't know what kind of relationship you have with your mother, but that's the only reason I haven't found her and put a bullet through her fuckin' skull," he said through gritted teeth. "She's the scum of the earth in my eyes. You don't keep a man and his children apart and for that, she will forever be dead to me. I'm not allowing another minute to pass us by, and I promise you that. I love you Messiah and you'll never know another day without me. That's on my life." He hugged me tightly and I embraced him. Hugging another grown man was weird for me but it also was something I knew we both needed. We had a moment that I appreciated more than he would ever know.

"Thanks." I walked out not knowing if *thanks* was the right response or how to feel about everything he said. My mother still wasn't answering her phone or calling me back and my granny was on mute about the whole situation which only meant she knew more than she was willing to say. Before she would ever think about lying to us about anything, she always hit us with her famous line, *"ask ya momma."*

143

Shaking off my thoughts of Mauricio and Charlene, I shot Giz a text with all the addresses that Smitty had just passed over. My hope was that between Giz tech guys and mine, we should be able to narrow down a location. We had to get Alyssa away from these niggas and quick. He's proven one too many times that he gives less than a fuck, and I couldn't allow him to play with her life, especially since she's pregnant.

****

Everyday Jaxsyn's progress was getting better and better, and she was even surprising the doctors. We'd turned everything she needed to relearn into a game. Making it fun took the stress out of it and reduced the number of times she would get overwhelmed and frustrated. Her determination to get better and learn more was beyond impressive and I was so proud. She was fighting and we were all fighting with her. Even our babies were helping their mommy and it meant the world to me to know that we were raising incredible children.

Since Jaxsyn's condition was improving, Brian came to me and said he and Kabrina thought it was time to tell her about Sydnee. Although I didn't agree, I knew it was just me trying to protect her from the pain that I was all too familiar with. Losing Nash dismantled my heart, and I didn't want Jaxsyn to endure that kind of pain. With everything she's been through, this blow could be the setback that takes her away from me again. She used to change Sydnee's diapers, do her hair, tease her all the time. We all knew she would be crushed, but they didn't see her breakdown weeks ago after we watched our children get taken out of our home. Jax lost it and I couldn't allow that to happen again. She needed to hear this from me, but it was imperative to choose my words wisely and delicately to ease the blow.

Pulling Jaxsyn into my arms, I watched her as she slept. She looked peaceful with her head lying on my chest. Every now and then she has nightmares and they always throw off the balance we're trying to reintroduce to her life. Brian wants her to get therapy, but I don't know how she would feel about that considering how everything went down with Rebecca. She confided in her for years and she used the information against her. For now, my arms was going to bring my Tink comfort.

"Hey beautiful." I stroked the side of her face as she slowly started to wake up.

"Hey you." She stretched and searched my eyes. I'm not sure what she was looking for, but her face scrunched up. "Wh what's wrooong?" She said slowly and then looked around for the kids. I saw her start to panic, and immediately put her mind at ease, letting her know the kids were with her parents down the hall. I could see her relax and I didn't want to get her worked up again, but I couldn't be a pussy. I had to tell her.

"I need to talk to you baby." I kissed her lips and she smiled pulling me closer. She's been horny as fuck since she's been awake, and I found it hilarious that through everything she was still my same ol' Jax. "You crazy." I pecked her again and then got serious. "I have to tell you something and no matter how much it hurts, you need to know that I'll be right by your side every step of the way."

"Oooh God." Her eyes filled with tears and she braced herself. "Myyy momma?"

"No. She's getting better every day and about to head to rehab in a couple days. She'll be down here to see you soon. I told you that's where the kids are." I brought her closer and kissed her again. "It's Sydnee baby." She gasped as tears instantly poured from her eyes and sadness replaced the sparkle that was just there.

"What?" She asked and I cautiously explained the whole situation to her. She wailed as I held her as tightly as I could. I also told her about Alyssa being missing since that text didn't come until after the accident, so she didn't know that either. If I had to break her heart than it was best to do it all at once instead of telling her about Syd, and then later on telling her that Lyss was missing or worse.

After telling Jax about Lyss, I knew she instantly felt guilty and when she asked for Dawson and Jagger it confirmed what I assumed. They had been keeping their distance because of howJax felt after she found out about Rebecca but as soon as I called them, they were walking into her room. They're normally in the lobby out of respect for how she felt but their love for her wouldn't allow them to go any further than that. They understood her position and respected it, but they weren't leaving her no matter how much she pushed.

I walked out and gave them a moment because when Jax saw them, she became unhinged again. I knew she was in good hands, so I allowed them time to grieve their little sister together. I sent Zionna a text letting her know I'd told Jax and to check on her when she got a chance. She had been with Fresh a lot lately which caused friction between us, so I wasn't surprised when she didn't text me back. It was far more important things happening in my world than Fresh and Z. I love that Jax had a moment with my brother when she was in the coma and that's beautiful, but his blessing from the other side didn't have shit to do with me and my loyalty. The shit between Fresh and Z was tasteless, and I spoke on it. Shit, they grown and can do whatever they want, but I didn't have to like or accept it.

Jaxsyn

My mother was leaving to go to rehab today and everything about this scene gave me flashbacks. I had watched her go to rehab so many times as I kid, and every time she went, I prayed that the outcome would be different. Every time, I prayed that "this time" would be the time that she really did it, that she really got better for me and although she would last longer than Sandy and give me and Z a glimpse of a normal life, that's all it ever was. A glimpse. She never stayed sober long enough for neither her nor I to fully enjoy her sobriety. She could never kick her habit and now that I know why she couldn't, the shit hurts like hell. For years I hated my mother and felt less than, because I begged her to just do it for me, and she had done it for me. Several times. Unbeknownst to her, the deck was stacked against her and we both paid dearly.

She refused to leave the hospital without seeing me first and I was happy she did. I hadn't seen her since I woke up from the coma I was in and for some reason I was yearning for her touch. I needed my momma, and I hadn't felt that way in years. I don't know if it was because of everything that I was going through with my health or the guilt of putting Rebecca before her, all these years. Either way, I needed her near and as soon as she walked into my room, we both broke down crying and she held me in her arms.

"You're so strong my precious baby. This won't beat you, Jax. You're going to make a full recovery and be a better mom to those babies than I ever was." She kissed the bandages on my head repeatedly as I held on to her every word. She prayed over me as her touch brought me peace. A sense of peace that I had never felt before, not even with Messiah or my daddy. Her love for me radiated off of her and consumed me.

"I… I'm so sor--"

"Unt uh. No ma'am. There will be none of that. You have nothing to apologize to me for. At all." She made me look at her and she looked so beautiful, nothing like when I first found her on that basement floor. "I could always see the evil in Rebecca, and I was always very vocal about that, but I could also see the love she had for you. I was jealous for many years, and many reasons, but my parents always taught me to trust my gut because it'll never lie to me. I knew what I felt towards her was more than just the typical jealousy, I had no idea why though. I absolutely hate what she's put all of us through. Her actions caused me to miss years with my only child but at the same time, I can't ignore nor forget that she was there for you when I was too out of my mind to be the mother you deserved. Had I not been on drugs in the first place, she wouldn't have had a weapon to use it against me, so I take full responsibility for my actions. No matter how guilty she is, I will always have respect for her. I wasn't so jealous or high that I didn't realize her position in your life. She deserved how you treated her and so did I." Tears streamed down her face.

"No. You tried to get off drugs so many times ma. I remember, I would only get a few sober days out of you before Sandy showed up with drugs. Knowing that she was only showing up because she was jealous of you and my daddy's bond and the fact that Rebecca was supplying her with drugs to keep you hooked, is unforgivable." I took a deep breath because talking was so strenuous for me.

"I understand you're on this new journey of forgiving and being a better person and I'm here for that, you know I am. I just can't be there with you. I hate her for everything she's done and yes, I do need to apologize. If not for you, then for me. I'm so sorry for the harsh things I said whether they were true or not. You're my mother and I love you to death." She was crying so hard that it made me start crying too. I stuttered the whole time I was talking but I had to get this out, whether I struggled through it or not. I could tell her tears were for both what I said but also for the condition I was in. I knew as hard as it was for me to deal with the confusion and having to learn everything all over again or be reminded of certain things, it was also hard for the people around me too. It's never easy watching someone you love go through any kind of hardship and this was definitely that for me.

She took a deep breath and told me she loved me too. We both escaped into our own thoughts for a moment before she started talking again, "Today is our new beginning. We're going to focus on starting fresh and pushing forward. When I get through this rehab again, and you get through your physical therapy, we're going to finally live our best lives, together." I nodded and hugged her tightly. I didn't want her to go, and she gave me as much time in her arms as I needed. I cried for what seemed like an hour and she shooed everyone away that tried to tell her it was time for her to go. With everything I've been through with my momma, I never needed her more than this moment and I felt blessed that she was sober enough to give it to me. Her words were exactly what I've yearned for my whole life and her presence brought the perfect peace to the storm I was in. "I'm so sorry about your sisters' baby. They're going to find Alyssa soon so don't you worry. I want you focused on getting better for my grand babies." She rubbed my head gently as I nestled into her embrace. She rocked me like a baby and slowly my eyes became heavy, and I fell asleep crying in her arms.

When I woke up, Zionna was sleeping on the couch with the girls stretched out all the way across her, and Messiah was standing by the window with Junior laying against his chest. Watching him with our son brought tears to my eyes. Sih was a man of his word and even when he doubted himself, I never doubted him. I knew he would find our baby one way or another or he would burn this city down trying. That kind of security in a man was something that I was still getting used to. I spent years with Black and never felt an inkling of what Messiah brought into my world. I knew my life and my children's lives were safe with him and I silently thanked God for that kind of security.

He must have felt me looking at him because he turned around and his eyes landed on mine causing a smile to slowly creep across his face. Lord he's beautiful. His hair was freshly lined up and braided, his beard looked shiny and luxurious, and his body looked amazing in the white tank he was wearing. I've peeped the nurses smiling in his face but one thing I never had to worry about and that was another bitch. I knew for a fact that his eyes were for me and only me.

"He was fighting his auntie on going to sleep so I had to step in." He kissed Junior's head as he laid him in their bed that he had setup in my room.

"He just wanted his daddy's arms," I said and we both jumped from shock. That was the clearest thing I had said since I opened my eyes. Every single day was a struggle for me. Literally, every single day. Some days I would get so frustrated with just trying to get my mouth and mind to work together that I would just give up and not say shit at all and the moment I would give up, my babies would say something to me or encourage me with their little voices causing me to go harder.

"Wooow Baby." Messiah kissed me deeply. "How the fuck am I this blessed to have a woman like you?" I smiled and hunched my shoulders playfully as he climbed into my bed. "That was amazing baby."

"Thank. You," I said slowly and got comfortable in his arms. "Talk to me." I stroked his beard and listened to his heartbeat. He was calm but I could tell his thoughts were heavy.

"I just want you to focus on getting better so we can get you home baby. Nothing else matters."

"Don't do that." I shook my head. "Talk."

He chuckled slightly and kissed my head. "I have to get Alyssa away from this crazy muthafucka, Baby. Every day that I don't find her is another day that he could be doing anything to her and that shit haunts me at night. I said one too many times that we're done with taking losses only for us to turn around and take another fuckin' L." I sat up and faced him before placing my head against his.

"Breathe." I closed my eyes after he closed his and I stroked his head gently. "You… got… this… Daddy." He nodded and I took my place back in his arms. I knew he had our world resting firmly on his shoulders but all he had to do was relax and refocus as usual. Messiah always feels as though he can solve the world's problems and as much as I love that about him, that's far too much pressure for one person and I couldn't have this cruel ass world or our current situation, breaking my baby down. That wasn't even an option.

****

Sleep didn't come easy for me these days. If I wasn't worried about my health, then I was weighed down by the guilt I felt when it came to my sisters. Sydnee told me that she felt I treated Alyssa better and I promised her that I would do better. Then I turned right around and shunned her at the first sign of trouble. I didn't shy away from the fact that I didn't want her, Dawson, and Jagger in my home because of their mother. Not once did I try to understand how hard it must have been for all of them to hear that their mother did the things that she did, but also that our father never even really loved Rebecca and had

151

been cheating on her for years. I selfishly grouped them in with her and shut down. Now my baby sister was fuckin' gone and I can never apologize for my behavior or tell her how much I love her.

Every time I close my eyes, I see her face and guilt washes over me. I can't get the memories of us growing up out of my head. Knowing that she wanted me to be more involved in her life and that opportunity had been ripped away from us damn near crushed my soul daily. She hadn't even begun to really live her life before it was taken from her. I was physically ill with trying to wrap my mind around her being gone.

The guilt I felt about Sydnee was the same guilt I felt when it came to Alyssa. I was so nasty towards Alyssa when she didn't deserve my anger at all. I've never talked to her the way that I did at Daulph's house and I prayed so hard that God gave me the opportunity to-

"Excuse me Mr. Knight, there's a Lace Patterson here to see you."

I was instantly pissed. This bitch was really trying it. I let her ass make it before because we had deeper shit going on that needed to be addressed, but her showing up here was definitely a sign of disrespect. I didn't give a fuck what was happening in those streets, her showing up to this hospital was too much. I immediately felt like she was trying to flex her position in Messiah's life by breaking protocol and doing her own thing. Not even Solo would have just showed up at the hospital without calling or texting first, but this bitch thought she just had free reign and she didn't.

He exhaled and stood up. Before I could even address him about the situation, he made his way over to my bed and kissed me.

"I knew she was coming, baby. Something happened and I didn't want her telling me over the phone. I'll be right back." He kissed me again and I just stared at him. "I know, Tink." He smirked and shook his head. "I love yo' crazy ass."

"Mmhmm." I gave him the finger causing us both to laugh. I knew I didn't have to worry about him doing anything with her or no shit like that, but I've always been huge on respect and this hoe had none. I don't care if he asked her to come here or not. I didn't want her nowhere near me and my family.

"Hey, Boo." Zionna walked in and I pointed to the door. "Yeah, that hoe still out there if that's what you're asking. Whatever she's telling Sih has him pissed the fuck off. How long they been out there?"

"Just… now."

"Oh okay. Well, if his ass is out there too long, I'll go check on them." I smiled as she flared her nostrils and poked her lips out. "You already know." She rolled her eyes before we both laughed, and she started telling me about how she couldn't sleep because Syd was heavily on her mind. She was feeling guilty too and I slowly explained to her that I felt the same way.

Sih walked back into the room with his phone to his ear and fire in his eyes. Without him saying a word I knew that Gato had struck again and whatever he did had my baby steaming. He barked orders to whoever he was speaking to on the phone and then turned to me.

"I have to go but I'll be back. Z stay with her because I may not be back until late." He bent down and kissed the kids, but Junior wouldn't let him go. I watched him soften his expression and tone until he got our son to let him leave. He wouldn't tell me what happened, just that he'd explain later but he had to go and with that, he was out of the door. I had been a ball of emotions since I woke up and there was nothing I could do to control them. Tears rained down my face and Z simply hugged me and told me to trust Sih and know that he would always do whatever it took to make it back to me and the kids. Her words were true so I relaxed slightly and enjoyed the day with my sister and kids as much as I could, considering…

Mauricio Vargas

This notion that I had been in hiding was complete bullshit and something that my brother Fernando knew was a lie before it even left his mouth. He wished that I was hiding to make his scary ass look better, but that's never been the case. Now, did I stay out of the spotlight? Yes. I'm a very powerful man and all my moves have to be well thought out and meticulous just to ensure that I make it through the day. The amount of weight I move from country to country makes me a moving target every time I leave the house. My dealings are international and on a level that my brother could never relate to, with some of the most dangerous people on the planet. If I'm not cautious, I'm dead, and those are the rules of the game.

Smitty was absolutely right, my brother has always been and forever will be jealous of me. Craziest part about his feelings towards me is that I've never wanted anything more than to love his punk ass our whole life. For years I hated that I was too young to follow behind my brothers but eventually I developed a love for tagging along with my father. His friends embraced me more than kids my age. I sat around nothing but knowledge and wisdom as I listened to their stories and soaked up the gems they were dropping. They taught me to be sagacious and sharp. As time passed, I held on to a piece of all of them, latched on to my father's ways, and followed in his footsteps. Jose and Fernando were still hanging out with friends and found pleasure in simple shit like chilling at the mall, while I was sitting amongst millionaires picking their brains on how they got to where they were and how I could get there. My father fuckin' loved my hunger and willingness to learn which made it easy for him to groom me.

When my father came to all three of us and told us it was time to step up in the Cartel, I was the first in line to do my part. Fernando being the oldest tried to flex his muscles and send me out to New York to handle the prostitution ring because to him, that was a low-level position. He hated how much my father and I had bonded over the years, not realizing he could have had that same bond, but they wanted to rip and run the streets chasing bitches instead of learning and chasing money like I did.

I went to New York and changed the whole face of what they had going on out there. My father was making thousands a week from the hoes he had, and I turned that shit into hundreds of thousands. I had bitches on the stroll, escorting, coming in from overseas and getting sent overseas. I was flippin' bitches like they were in Detroit flippin' bricks. Our father's chest swelled with pride, further pissing Fernando off.

At the height of my New York stint, I met Charlene. She had been working for me for a couple years, but I was young and getting money in a city that never sleeps. I had so many bitches I couldn't even remember most of their names. I had the hoes I was selling plus the bitches I was fuckin' which I sometime turned into hoes to be sold too. If the pussy hit right all I could see was dollar signs and if she gave me the okay, I'd put her ass to work. I never forced women to do anything. I paid well and kept my hands off of them, so they came willingly.

Charlene was special. She was what most pimps call a "bottom bitch." I never thought of myself as a pimp, I've always been an entrepreneur. I provided a service for a fee and that service just happen to come from a willing woman. I didn't take more than half and make all kinds of demands. I provided a safe environment for adults to be adults, and everyone came out happy. Charlene saw how different I was, and she started going above and beyond to please me. I noticed the effort she was putting forth and

156

after a few weeks of her bending over backward to get my attention that she already had, I gave her the dick she wanted. Her pussy was a gold mine. To date, her pussy is the only pussy that comes close to my wife and considering how many bitches I fucked when I was living wild out here, that says a lot. We were fuckin' like rabbits and spending a decent amount of time together. I can't say I ever loved her, but I damn sure cared about her and she made a mark on my life.

Shit was going too well, so of course something had to happen. My father's health took a turn for the worst and right after his health started failing, my mother had a heart attack. She shook up our whole world because she damn near didn't make it. There was too much going on and my father decided it was time to step down and take care of his health and his wife. He sent my mother back to Colombia and started getting his affairs in order. As a gift to him I surprised him the night before he retired with six duffle bags of nothing but hundreds. He stared at me with a confused expression on his face before he smirked.

"What is this, son?"

"Part of August profits. I wanted to personally deliver it to you. That's one million in cash off of one month." I smiled from ear to ear and his smirk turned into a full-blown laugh.

"You're something else." He nodded. "You make me a proud father. I always knew you would." He got up from his desk and hugged me tightly. We shared a moment of love and admiration that we'd never shared, and when he let me go, he told me to keep the money. "Well deserved." He patted my back and I nodded because I was choked up. Him being proud of me meant the world to me. I'd worked damn hard and to hear this pride filled man tell me that he was proud was amazing, it's a moment I'll never forget.

The next day he announced his retirement and named me as his successor. It was no surprise to anyone because I had put in the work. I was my father's shadow. The Cartel was calling for me to take his place when he stepped down for years and often people joked about it, so no one but my brothers were surprised. Fernando acted as if it was a slap in the face. He automatically assumed because he was the oldest that he was just supposed to rightfully step into the head role, and it baffled me. This muthafucka had a lot of nerve but I wasn't fazed by his outburst and bullshit.

My father on the other hand, after weeks maybe months of Fernando's adult tantrums over not getting chose, my father pulled me to the side telling me that he needed to bring peace to the family, and he was going to agree with my decision to step down. I had told him a week into the position that I would step down to silence his son, but he ignored me. I knew eventually his hand would get forced because I knew Fernando. I heard the whispers about my brothers making threats on my life, and if I'd heard them so did our father. I could sell water to a whale though, so I wasn't the least bit moved by the decision we made for me to step down or the threats. My father didn't want shit to happen between us or any internal wars to be started so he did what any father would do, he called an audible, mid-play.

Fernando immediately started trying to call shots and do what he assumed bosses do. I laughed at his ass like he was a joke because in reality, that's exactly what he was. I went back to New York for a while but shit between us only got worse. Distance couldn't even mend what was broken between us. My father moved back to Colombia and that's when shit really took a turn. My brother really started trying to call shots that didn't need to be called and I wasn't going for it. I was trying to build wealth and live a good life while this muthafucka wanted accolades and recognition for the half ass shit he was doing. He surrounded himself with a bunch of yes men like Smitty and they had him thinking he was a big shit.

Around this time, I started dating my now wife, Destiny. I had never seen a woman more beautiful, and I knew once she gave me a chance I couldn't it fuck up. She played hard to get for a while because her father was the pastor of a popular Baptist church and it was no secret who I was and what I did. We creeped for quite a while until she built up enough courage to introduce us and as soon as she did, I cut everyone off including Charlene. I knew Destiny's love for the Lord and her family might keep us apart but once she threw caution to the wind, I locked her down. Her family loved me and never judged me for what I did in the street. We were the happiest we've ever been when my brother tried to make me come back to Detroit and do his grunt work. I wasn't doing it and I was vocal about it. The threats became harsher and eventually the noise I was hearing about them having a price on my head *again* became too loud to ignore. I reached out to my homie who is an architect and told him I needed a low-key spot in Miami built from the ground up.

When we got to Miami a couple months later, they still needed time to complete our home, so I got us a little condo to be comfortable in until our home was finished. I was bouncing back and forth between Miami, New York, and Detroit handling business. I had a hand in several different illegal businesses while also getting my feet wet with legal ventures as well. I had money coming at me from every direction and I was trying to get it all.

I finally kicked it with Fernando on some man-to-man shit about parting ways and he acted as if everything was cool. We could no longer do business and I didn't need a war with everything I was trying build. I went back to Miami and shit between me and Des started getting bad. She told me that she was pregnant and wanted me to slow down but when I didn't, she went back to New York. I

159

chased her for a couple months, but I didn't want to stress her and my baby out so I focused on the streets and stacking my bread. I ran into Charlene on some random shit one night and popped her off for old time's sake. Shit had me missing her ass but Destiny had my heart, so I cut all ties with Charlene after that night.

Two months before Des was due, Jose shot my ass and left me for dead. Never in my life did I imagine my brother shooting me but that was my fault, I had been warned. He left my ass to bleed out, not giving one fuck that I was his brother or that I had a kid on the way. By the time I got out of the hospital, our home was done and furnished. Destiny didn't leave my side the whole time and I knew I was going to marry her. After she gave birth to my son, I proposed, and we got married a month later. I've been getting money and taking care of my family ever since, and then I randomly get a phone call from Giz telling me I have two sons that I didn't know shit about, and my brother was behind one of them getting killed. After I got off the phone I cried like a bitch. My first-born son didn't even get a chance to find out that I didn't know about him and I wasn't just some pussy ass guy that ran out on his momma. That shit hurt to my core.

I refused to allow my brother to take another person that I love and I had him right in my sights making sure that didn't happen. I know Messiah wants to handle this shit alone and every time I offer to help, I can tell he gets tense because he doesn't know if he can fully trust me or not but every day I try to prove to him that I'm here and I'm never going anywhere. He's my baby boy and I'll go through hell and high water to make sure not a hair on his head or the heads of his family get touched.

"Baby this is amazing." My wife Destiny smiled and I shook my head.

"Don't you go getting any ideas woman."

"Hush. I'm not." She continued happily looking around the Estate and I have to admit, this was pretty fuckin' amazing. When Messiah told me everything that happened in his home, I knew he had to protect his family better. I called my homie that night and told him what I needed. He found a mansion that was already in production that was on the market. The builders stopped building when the people that hired them couldn't afford to finish the job. We swooped right in and sealed the deal. I had my friend add to it and secure it the same way he did our home in Miami. "When can I meet them? You keep saying soon."

"I don't want to intrude, Baby. They have a lot going on. I don't want to overwhelm him. Hell, he doesn't even acknowledge Carmine."

"Well, that's because he doesn't want to feel like he's cheating on his brother with another brother, Baby."

I stared at her in amazement. I loved this woman with everything inside of me. Where I lack, she's right there to fill in. I hadn't thought about that, but she was a hundred percent correct.

"You're right."

"Always." She smiled. "Now call him so I can meet my grand babies and my daughter-in-law. Carmine's mean butt is not going to give us either, anytime soon."

"Right again." We both laughed as I locked up the home I had built for my son and his family. I could only hope its beauty draws them in as it did us and didn't make them feel like I'd over stepped. I wasn't trying to buy Messiah's love at all, but he's my son and I want him and his family safe. The only way I could ensure that was to do it myself.

Messiah didn't answer his phone so I decided to just go up to the hospital like I normally would. I had been visiting Jax a lot since she woke up and she was always happy to see me. I prayed over her night and day. She didn't deserve to go through what she was going through and I had a team working with her at the hospital and another team waiting for her to be discharged.

I nodded towards my security as Destiny, and I walked up. The police hadn't been lurking lately and my lawyers were working hard to keep it that way. We needed to find whoever this Toya bitch is and handle her so this shit could go away permanently. Until then, my lawyers will have DPD tied up in litigations over how they treated Jaxsyn as she fought for her life.

"Hello, beautiful ladies." I spoke and both Jaxsyn and her sister Zionna smiled.

"Hey, Mauricio." They said in unison and the kids started running to me, so I rushed to swoop my grandson in my arms. On the regular he pushes his leg to the limit, and it was hindering it from healing properly.

"This is my wife, Destiny, Des this is Jaxsyn, her sister Zionna, and my munchkins Nevaeh, Jeniah, and Junior."

"So nice to meet you all." Destiny went around hugging everybody. The only one that wasn't receptive was Jeniah, but she was like that with me too. Jaxsyn said she's a diva and has to warm up to new people and she definitely warmed up to me like she said she would, so I told Des the same thing.

"Where's Messiah?" I asked as I played with the kids. They always lit up time I walked into a room and every time they did I was a proud Papa.

"I don't know. Lace showed up with bad news a little while ago which only means Gato has done something else to make our lives a living hell. Sih started yelling at people over the phone and then said he'd be back. I haven't heard from him since."

I nodded in response, kissed the kids, and told the women I would be back too. Des wanted to stay and Jaxsyn was cool with it, so I told her I'd send a car for her later. I needed to be wherever my son was. I called Giz to find out what was going on and within no time me and Carmine were pulling up, ready for whatever.

Messiah

Every single dollar, pill, and medical supply that was stolen from my Georgia warehouse and my shipping trucks, was dropped off at The Knights headquarters twenty minutes before the DEA arrived. Solo and Fresh just happened to be there and knew immediately that some bullshit was about to go down and swiftly handled that shit. Every club house and warehouse that I have is equipped to handle situations like this by my Knights that's in the loop on the illegal shit.

Unfortunately, because everyone was so focused on hiding the shit that can get you locked up for football numbers, they didn't hide the weapons that they had on them. The good thing was none of the guns had a body on them or no shit like that, but not all of them were registered. Considering the fact that they could have been caught with millions in unexplainable money, medicine, and medical equipment, I still think they made out good. I gave one of my prospects the money to go bail everyone out and then went up to my office to breathe.

Today could have been worse than it was, and it almost felt like a win. Those didn't come our way that often and I just needed a minute to appreciate that we acted fast and escaped what could have had the potential to really hit us hard. Everybody in this bitch would have went down including the members that don't have the slightest clue on what happens in the background. That shit wouldn't have been a good look at all, and the attention would have fell right on me. My name is all I have, and I would have been dragged through the mud, when The Knights have always been a positive force in my community. It's why Nash and I worked so hard to keep our two worlds completely separated. The legal business dealings that I worked hard to secure took a hit when I went to jail but Jaxsyn salvaged most of them. This whole situation would have killed that shit. These niggas were gunning for my life from every angle.

"Come in," I said loud enough for Mauricio to hear me. I saw him walking up from the security cameras that I had up on my laptop.

"You good?" His hands were tucked into his pockets and he looked nervous. I knew he felt responsible for the shit that was poppin' off in my life and rightfully so. Shit, these niggas were coming at me, to get to him, but I didn't blame him. He didn't have to feel whatever he was feeling.

"Just ready to end these muthafuckas. I feel like I sound like a broken record every time some shit goes down. I'm telling my people shit like *don't worry* and *we gone catch these clowns,* but they just keep coming at us harder and harder and I can't lie, I'm tired as fuck. I been going for two years straight and it's catching up with me. I woke up from getting shot to an unimaginable reality that my brother was gone. Before I could even fathom that he was gone, my girl tells me that the police were trying to arrest me. Same hoe ass shit they did to her too. Except I'll die before I allow them to sit her down for that Mariah shit." I shook my head just thinking about her going to jail. We'll go on the run before that shit ever happens. Ain't no way in hell she's going through that. "I served fifteen months and missed out on the majority of her pregnancy plus the kids birth. She deserved better than that from me and I failed her. Come out to my kids getting snatched up and my maid that was a really close friend getting killed in my crib causing my girl to have a fuckin' nervous breakdown.

Again, they all deserved better than that. My life went from sugar to shit and it's just getting shittier as the days go by. I ain't never in my life felt this fuckin' out of control and it's killing me. All the fuck I want is to raise my children away from all this bullshit and make my girl my wife." I took a deep breath. I ain't no weak ass nigga but I was beyond tired. I didn't have twenty-five plus years to give to these Vargas's like Mauricio. I wasn't in this for the long haul. I wanted revenge on these muthafuckas and then to move on with my life.

"Son, everything that has happened to you is lying at my feet. Nothing that has transpired in the last two years was your fault and I can't apologize to you and your family enough. Fernando is a problem that I should have been solved and although I know you want his blood on your hands and you feel as though this is personal for you, imagine how I feel. He's been doing this shit to me since we were kids. I'm a fifty-six-year-old man now, and he's passed that hate down to my children. He is the reason Nashon is gone and for that, more than anything else, he's done to me, he will pay. Your brother may be gone Messiah but you're not alone in this."

"Yeah, well, I'm just the only one taking losses in this whole shit so it definitely feels like I'm alone. He was your son, but you didn't know him. My big brother was my fuckin' world. I don't know this fuckin' life without him and I'm grasping at fuckin' straws trying to get through this shit without him." I felt myself getting emotional and that's not what I was trying to be on right now. Once again, it was time to think of my next move to get me closer to these niggas and figure out how to get Alyssa back while making sure Jax and the kids are no longer in the line of fire.

Now that the DEA had been called, I already knew they were going to be watching us like a fuckin' hawk, so I also had to figure out how to get the meds and money out of here undetected. The last thing we need is some rookie ass agent with a hard on for us, bringing his ass back to dig deeper.

"Carmine and I will never replace Nash in your life Messiah and neither of us is trying to, we're family though and family is everything to me. Your losses are our losses, son. When you're hurting, like right now, I can feel that shit and as your parent I want to fix it. Especially because this has nothing to do with you and--"

"It has nothing to do with you either." We both looked towards the door and a short man that I immediately knew was my grandfather started walking towards us.

"Papi?" Mauricio sounded choked up as he met him in the middle of the floor and bear hugged him. They held each other for a while before letting go. "What are you doing here?"

"Destiny called me. Son, you should have been called. I had no idea all of this was happening." His voice held so much pain in it I could feel it from across the room. "I loss a grandson that I didn't even know about and you didn't even call your mother and I to tell us."

"It's not like that. I didn't know about them until their cousin called me, and by then, Nashon was already gone. This is my other son, Messiah."

"Well, I know that now because I did my own research." He walked over to me and before I could stand to greet him, he kissed both sides of my face. I didn't know how to accept that, so I just stared at him. "You look just like your grandmother. She has those same hazel brown eyes. She's going to love you." He patted my back and turned back to Mauricio. "He's done. This has nothing to do with him and everything to do with you and I. Fernando has always been jealous and your mother and I thought he would grow out of it, but he hasn't, and now he's gone too far." He took a seat and motioned for my father to do the same with a nod of the head. "My grandson will not fight your battles. He has too much to lose and has already lost too much. I want Fernando and Dominic in my face by the end of the week and that's an order." His tone dripped hate and I know from having children that I'll do anything and everything to give them the world so to go from that feeling to straight up hate must be a hard pill to swallow.

"I have eyes on Fernando as of last night. I had someone sitting on your estate because I had a feeling he was hiding out there but then Smitty confirmed it. There hadn't been any movement until last night. My guys are almost positive it's him."

"You know I don't deal in possibilities, I deal in the definitive. Make sure it's him and bring his ass to me." He stared at Mauricio and he simply nodded. It was crazy to see how he was around his father opposed to how he carried himself on the regular. "Messiah, I want you with your family and nowhere else. I have someone snatching up the little bitch Toya that you've been looking for, tonight. She's in protective custody but I pulled some strings, and we have her location. As soon as she's out of the picture so are the allegations. That woman of yours is deadly and I want to meet her soon. I saw the case files on your ex, and I like her style." He chuckled to himself causing me to smirk because Jax was definitely a force. "Dominic was behind the heist in Georgia, but it was the little bitch Lace that's downstairs barking orders that put the call in to the DEA. She's working with my grandson to take you down and she'll be dealt with shortly."

"I appreciate--" He held his hand up.

"You lost your brother behind our shit, your kids were taken, your woman is laid up in the hospital, her sister was killed, another missing…" He took a deep breath and exhaled. "This is on us and as bad as you may want revenge, this is our battle to fight, you just happened to get caught in the crosshairs. I'm going to make sure you get to avenge your family but step back for a minute and allow us to take it from here. Jaxsyn and your children need a hundred percent of you right now and you can't give them that and track down your cousin that's trying to kill you."

He stood up. "I already spoke to Giz and Fresh about Toya and they told me where to bring her once we have her in our possession. She'll be waiting for you when you're ready." His eyes landed on Mauricio. "Call your mother and let her know I didn't put my hands on you. If you try some shit like this again, you may not be so lucky. Together we could have had this taken care of weeks ago, but your pride kept you from reaching out. Your hate for your brother had you moving recklessly, and too many people suffered for it. I taught you better than that, now act like it." He was poking him in his chest and then walked away.

"I think I just saw my daddy get a spanking," I said as soon as my grandfather left the room and we both died laughing. It was a much-needed laugh, and it came straight from both of our guts. I don't know why but I trusted them despite all the snake shit that was happening around me. I felt content knowing that they would be handling shit behind the scenes and I could focus on my family for a minute. That's where I was needed most.

I looked at the security cameras just as one of Mauricio's guys put his hand over Lace's face and she immediately collapsed in his arms. He swiftly picked her up like a feather and carried her out without anyone even noticing. It was so smooth that it caused me to chuckle to myself.

"Chloroform. Consider her taken care of." We both got up to leave. "I'm really sorry, son."

"Stop. Let's just bring this shit to an end so I can start the next chapter of my life with my babies."

"Speaking of next chapters." He pulled out a key. "Jaxsyn said they're releasing her in a couple day so me and Des wanted to do something special for you and the family to start over fresh. I'll text you all the information." He hugged me and I thanked him. I didn't know what to expect but I appreciated him for everything he was doing.

Zionna

Two days in a row we couldn't get Jax to talk to anyone but the kids. She was on an emotional roller coaster. Some days she was okay, and others she was eerily in her feelings. She was hurting deeply, and it hurt that we couldn't help her. Brian hadn't been back to the hospital since Kabrina went to rehab and Jax felt like he was blaming her. I think he was just grieving his youngest child and worried about Jax and Alyssa's wellbeing. He had a lot on his plate too and although it seemed like he's avoiding her, I don't think that's the case at all.

I chose to give her and Messiah some space because every day she was backsliding more and more, and I knew if anyone could get her back on track it was him and the kids. She couldn't afford to move backwards at this point. She'd worked so hard, and she needed to keep that same energy going forward. I recognized her depression because I still battled with mine daily. I know my sister so I know she's going to shake back but seeing her pain and knowing there was nothing I could do to help her, hurt me.

"What's good, first lady?"

"That's Jaxsyn." I smiled at Solo as I sat down at the bar in the club house. I used to come here all the time, but it reminded me so much of Nash and the times we've spent making love in his office upstairs and just having the time of our lives in here. He loved The Knights with every fiber of his being and coming back here was always bittersweet.

"Nah. That's both of y'all. Nash and Sih ain't never split that Prez position in two. We never had a VP."

"Their love for each other was so real." I looked up at the picture hanging behind the bar of Nash and Sih on the day that they signed the papers for their first club house. That picture hangs in all of their clubs and warehouses. The genuine smiles on their faces brought tears to my eyes.

"*Is* so real." He corrected me. "He's still alive in our hearts. I know because I feel that nigga daily." Solo wrapped his arms around me, and I hadn't even noticed that I had started crying. This is why I stayed away most of the time but tonight I needed to feel close to him and this place, Solo, and the rest of the guys always made me feel more connected to him.

I kicked it with Solo for a little while before I went up to Nashon's office. I walked in and placed my back against the door. Two years and it still smelled like him. My eyes watered as I took in what used to be my favorite place. A smile crept over my face as the tears that were threatening to fall slide down my cheeks. I thought back on how his wild ass used to bend me over his desk every chance he got. From day one he was the right amount of thug and gentleman. He would yank my head back like a fuckin' savage and then whisper softly in my ear "Tell a nigga you love him" and each time I said it I could feel him getting harder inside of me. Damn… I missed his ass so fuckin' much.

I ran my fingers alongside his desk and the tears kept coming but they weren't bad tears persè. I just missed my man and thinking about our memories had me wanting him near me. I sat down in his chair and laid my head back. So much was going on around me and all I wanted was his touch or for him to tell me that everything would be alright. As crazy as he was, his ass brought a calmness to my life that I never expected. He didn't sweat small shit and he didn't let me sweat it either and when the big shit occurred, he took the same approach. "You can't trip over shit you can't control baby" is what he would always say. I needed that right now.

"Hey. Solo told me you were up here, so I just wanted to check on you. You straight?" Fresh had his head peeked inside of the door and I shook my head no. He came in and I cried in his arms. All I wanted was shit to go back to the way it was. Out of all the no-good people in this world, why did God choose Nashon? His heart was so pure, and he didn't have an ill bone in his body. He helped people every single day of his life. Yet, he's gone and muthafuckas like Gato were still roaming around freely. It just didn't make sense and my heart couldn't take it.

"I miss him so much."

"I know you do but you know like I know, he wouldn't want you in here crying like this." He rubbed my back and I nodded. Nash was always about having a good time so I knew he wouldn't want me constantly sulking over our memories. "Come on." Fresh stood me up and wiped my face. "You have a lot going on right now and you need to relax your mind." He took my hand before I could say anything, and we left out of my baby's office.

Two hours later, I felt absolutely amazing. Fresh took me to a five-star spa that pampered me like never before. Every inch of my body was relaxed, and my mind was at ease. From there he took me to have dinner and we talked all night. We end up staying at the restaurant until they closed. I needed the mental break that he provided, and I couldn't thank him enough. As we were walking out, I bumped right into Asia and Jared, Black's brother and sister. Many moons ago I dated Jared and then he started messing around with the big Debo acting ass bitch named Kim. That bitch was a fool over him and last I heard they had three kids together but she's in jail for fuckin' him and the kids up.

"Heeey, Boo." Asia hugged me and I waved to Jared.

"Hey, Love. Y'all been good?"

"Girl, yeah. Jared is always tied down with the kids so since they're all with Black and Ty tonight I decided to take him out for some fresh air."

"Well, that's good."

"Man, I heard about Jax and shit, we're praying for her to make a full recovery. No matter what, she's family." Jared said.

"I know and I'll tell her. I know she'll appreciate that coming from y'all."

"Fa'sho."

"Well, we'll let you go but make sure you tell my sis we're here if she needs us and sorry about the house. Shardae is back in jail and this time she's probably going to do some real time, so she doesn't have to worry about her looney ass anymore."

"Back in jail?"

"Yeah, after she burned the house down, they let her go for whatever reason, only for her to turn around and set their car on fire while they were out to eat. When they came outside, her and some niggas she know jumped them."

"Damn. That's crazy." I shook my head.

"Girl she found their new address and started fires in front of all the exits and threw a Molotov cocktail in the window. They asses barely made it out and that's why they're living with Jared for a minute. You know Ty's ass is pressing all the charges girl, to the fullest extent of the law. Okay!" We busted out laughing and then I cut the conversation short because Fresh had no clue what we were talking about and I didn't want to be rude.

As soon as we got in the car, I gave him the back story and we laughed at how hard karma was hitting Black's no good ass. He cheated and got that hoe pregnant behind my sisters back only for her to turn around and try to kill him and the nigga he was cheating on my sister with. It was hilarious and I texted my sister to make her laugh too, which she did. Her ass sent back so many laughing emojis that Fresh and I end up laughing about it all over again.

"I have to go check on some shit for Giz, but I hope I was able to turn your day around."

"You turn everyday around for me. I appreciate you so much."

"It's all good, Baby. I been there and grief will kill you if you allow it to."

"Man… don't I know it." I turned to look at him. "Thanks to you that's not an issue for me anymore."

We stared at each other before he told me he needed to get going and I nodded. I grabbed the handle to get out and he pulled me back, kissing me deeply and I needed his touch. I placed my hand on the back of his head and deepened it even more. Our tongues swirled in each other's mouths and this kiss was nothing like the mistake I made with Quan, this was something totally different. Something deeper. We slowly pulled apart and our heads rested against each other naturally and I swear our heartbeats filled the car that would have otherwise been quiet.

"I don't think that was a line we should have crossed, but I wanna cross it again," he said and I could tell he was battling himself. I hadn't told him about what Jax said but I couldn't get it off of my mind for a couple days after she said it. Messiah will just have to be mad because I yearned for the feeling that Fresh gave me and after all the shit I've been through in my life, I knew I deserved to be happy again. Instead of responding to him, I placed both of my hands on his face and started kissing him again. He pulled me closer, and I slowly made my way over the center console and into his lap. I fully welcomed whatever was happening between us and the way he was kissing and gripping me, he welcomed it too.

Rebecca

My thoughts had become full blown nightmares while I was wide awake. I couldn't catch a break, my mind raced with regrets constantly. I welcomed death with opened arms. My reality was far too harsh to live in and I was disgusted with myself and my actions over the years. The grief consuming me was something I had never felt in my life. My baby died a horrible death that could have been prevented if I wasn't such a horrible person. That's the part that cuts the deepest.

Jaxsyn is in the hospital fighting for her life, my grandson went flying through the windshield with her, Alyssa has been captured, and Syd was killed by her father. Yes, her father. I know I was wrong and I'm learning that sometime karma repays you through the people closest to you. I had no business crossing the line with Dominic when he was only a child. I couldn't keep my hands off of him, even though I knew I was wrong. One time turned into two, and before I knew it, we were sneaking around the house every day. I had him lying well and hiding what we shared like a pro. My patients told me stories that haunted them, similar to what I was doing to Dominic, and I still couldn't stop. Not even when I got pregnant with Syd. I told Brian I was pregnant, he had no reason to doubt the paternity, and I continued seducing my boyfriend's oldest child. The more my thoughts ran wild the more disgusted I became with myself.

I wanted nothing more than for Messiah to come back in here and put me out of my misery. I deserved the death that I knew he was going to deliver. Like I said, I welcomed it with a willing heart and opened arms. There was no denying I was going straight to hell and that's exactly where I deserved to be.

I heard a noise in the distance and prayed that it was Messiah or one of his people coming to finish me off. I didn't know how long I had been tied and bound in this room, but I knew it had been days. I was more than ready for his fury.

"Sshhhh." I heard feet coming my way and I braced myself since I couldn't see my death coming. I laced my fingers through each other and closed my eyes tightly. "Untie her and hurry up." Someone whispered and my body stiffened at the rough touch of whoever grabbed me. Seconds later my hands were free, and the blind fold was taken off of me. The light blinded me every time they removed my blindfold but this time my hands were free, so they instantly went towards my face to shield my eyes from the light. I felt my feet become free and I moved my hands.

"Are you okay? Did they hurt you?" Fernando pulled me into his arms, and I was confused and baffled. I broke down crying and he picked me up bridal style. "You're okay baby. I'm going to get you out of here. I'm so sorry Bec." Just as the words left his mouth and he started to walk, shots rang out. I ducked my head into his chest, and he started running with me in his arms. I felt like we were in an eighties action movie dodging bullets as his people shot back and the sound of ricocheting bullets caused us to flinch hoping we didn't get hit.

The nights air caught me by surprise because I didn't think we would make it out of there alive. I lifted my head as tears filled my eyes. I didn't deserve to be saved. I felt conflicted being in Fernando's arms. He was an evil man whom I wanted to hate so badly, but I also had a baby by his oldest son that I passed off as my husbands, so how could I judge… He placed my feet on the ground and my knees buckled. I hadn't stood in days and he caught me.

"Get down!" Someone yelled out as more shots started to rain down on us.

"Ahhhh." Fernando yelled out and several men started running towards us. They pushed both of us into his Cadillac truck and hit the gas so hard we all jerked. The firestorm didn't stop though. We were now being chased and I was shivering all over. I didn't know how to feel. Moments before Fernando showed up, I was praying for Messiah to come in and take me out of my misery and now that I was back with Fernando I was ducking down and praying not to get shot again. I still hadn't fully healed from the first time and now I was deathly afraid of that feeling coursing through my body again. "Fuuuck!" Fernando looked down at his bloody hand and laid his head back while closing his eyes. I put my hand on top of his wound and applied pressure. He winced in pain and gritted down on his teeth. "I'm sorry Rebecca."

"You're going to be okay Fernando."

He opened his eyes and stared at me. "He's losing control." He shook his head and chuckled to himself. "I created a monster."

"He killed my baby Fernando."

"I know…" He said barely above a whisper. "I would have never agreed to that no matter how mad I was at you and I hope you know that." He placed his bloody hand on top of mine. "He has Alyssa too, but I told him not to hurt her. I only wanted to teach you a lesson because I felt betrayed. I had no idea he was going to drop Sydnee from my fuckin' helicopter. I didn't find out until today and I knew I had to come get you because he's gone off the rail."

"How can you stop him?"

"I don't think that's possible. He's angry about his brother and I honestly think he's hurt by you leaving him that night, so he's lashing out like a fuckin' child."

"Watch out!" The guy in the passenger seat of the truck yelled out just as our truck swerved and we went barreling into a ditch. All of a sudden, the truck started rolling over and since none of us were wearing seatbelts, everyone and everything started flying everywhere. I was screaming at the top of my lungs but so were the men. This is not the death I was willing to accept. We flipped so many times the only reason I hadn't been ejected from the car is because I held on to the seat in front of me like I saw Fernando doing. The two guys in the front had been long gone and they were probably somewhere bleeding out. The truck finally flipped into a small river-like body of water, and we rushed to get out before we ended up trapped.

"Be careful, we have to--" His words were cut off by a shot to his shoulder. I looked behind me and a guy that looked exactly like Messiah was smirking at us and he had about ten men standing around him.

"Uncle Fernando. So nice to finally meet you." His smirk was menacing and sent a chill down my spine. "Today is going to be Christmas in the Vargas household. Grab these bitches and put them with the rest of the presents." He barked an order and before it was fully out of his mouth, a bag was placed over my head and I heard Fernando yelp in pain. This was about to get bad, really bad actually, and I couldn't stop wishing that he would have just left me where the fuck Messiah had me because these men seemed ten times worse. Once again, Fernando had screwed me without even pulling his dick out.

Jaxsyn

Messiah and I smiled from ear to ear as the doctor cut Junior's cast off. He'll still need to wear a leg brace for a couple weeks just because he's little and they want his leg to heal properly but he'll have more range and mobility to run around and play with his sisters. His little butt was cheesing hard too like he really knew what was going on. All he knew was now he didn't have to be "babied" as he called it and we could allow him to do what he wanted. I swear we have the smartest kids on the planet. They caught on to everything and were already strongly opinionated at their young ages. We were definitely going to have our hands full with this bunch.

"You ready, Tink? I already told the nurse to call transport and the doctor gave me your discharge papers."

"Definitely." I exhaled and laid my head back. I had been dressed all day because I knew they were taking Junior's cast off and discharging me today. I still wasn't sleeping well so when my dreams woke me up at five a.m. I just stayed up and waited for the sun to come up before I started stirring around. I could barely walk without my walker, but I asked Sih to start leaving it by the bed once they took my catheter out. That shit was painful as hell and I was so happy when they finally said I was strong enough to use the bathroom on my own. I had been begging to have it removed for weeks and they kept telling me no. No matter how many times Messiah said it was nothing to be embarrassed about, I definitely couldn't shake the embarrassment. I felt horrible every time he noticed the drainage bag was getting full and called the nurse to come switch the bag out. He acted as if it was nothing but to me it was degrading. I felt like an invalid and in more ways than one, I was. I had been robbed of being able to carry out basic daily functions and it killed me.

"Why are you this fuckin' beautiful Tink?" I blushed as Sih hovered over me.

"Stop. I… I look a mess."

"You always look perfect to me." He stroked the side of my face and then kissed me deeply. I wrapped my arms around his neck and deepened the kiss. His tongue weaved in and out of my mouth sensually and I was wet as hell, almost immediately. There was something about his touch that my body couldn't resist. When we slowly parted ways, I wanted more and he knew it so he smirked. "When we get home, I got you Baby." We both laughed.

I looked around the room that had become my home for the last few months and I couldn't wait to get the hell on but the thought of going back to the house that held so many horrors wasn't ideal either. If those walls could talk, they would have been screaming with the amount of shit that's happened in our home. Anything was better than the hospital though and I knew eventually we were going to move so I didn't even make a big deal out of it. Messiah still had a lot of shit going on in the streets, so I wasn't about to worry him over the small shit.

We waited almost an hour for transport to come escort me to the front of the building. I hated hospital protocol. My fiancé was more than capable to helping me downstairs, but hospital policy stated I had to be taken down in a wheelchair. Pen pushers always make the most stupid ass rules that we all have to follow because their lame asses think it's a good idea. Anyway, I was out, and the fresh air was everything. The sun hadn't touched my skin in what seemed like forever and Messiah gave me a minute to soak it all up.

"I have a surprise for y'all." He stood in the passenger side door after buckling my seatbelt. "You and the kids are going to love it." His smile brought a smile to my face even when I wanted no parts of smiling these days. I had so much on my mental that smiling seemed like a chore more than something normal that less fucked up humans did on the regular but whenever Messiah was in my presence I couldn't stop. His blemish free skin glowed in the sun as his brown eyes sparkled. His smile has always and will always be his most beautiful feature. I fell in love all over again and he could see it which made him smile harder. He leaned in and kissed me and told me that he loved me too.

"Kiss, Dada." Jeniah said and we both laughed. He went to the back and kissed both girls and Junior held his fist up to dap him. Sih laughed hysterically and both kissed and dapped Junior. He swore he was a big boy, and it was hilarious. Messiah wasn't having that shit though, Junior got the same kisses that his sisters got, and I loved it.

Our home was about an hour from the hospital, and we were now an hour and a half into what I started calling a road trip. I wondered where he was taking us, but I didn't say a word. I was happy to be free and my thoughts hadn't sucked me in yet, so I was calm and content. He reached for my hand and kissed the back of it as I smiled and enjoyed a taste of normality. We needed this, all five of us.

"Tink." I must have dozed off at some point. I opened my eyes, and we were still driving but he was slowing down.

"Where are we, Bae?" I finally asked as he started to turn.

"That came out really clear, Ma." He stroked the side of my face. I adored how attentive he was when it came to my progress. "We're home, baby." He nodded his head towards the window. I turned my head and gasped. Just as we passed an iron gate, the biggest and prettiest sign came into view, *Vargas-Knight Estate* and the street sign along the road we were traveling said Messiah Blvd. We kept going straight and the view was breathtaking. I could see a lake to the left of us and it was absolutely the most beautiful sight to see. Well, that was before we turned down Jaxsyn Way, and I placed my hand over my chest. No fuckin' way was this where we were going to live.

"Messiah."

"It's a newly built gift from Mauricio and Destiny. He gave me the keys a few days ago and I haven't been inside, but I drove up here the other day to see what it was. I couldn't believe it and I called and asked him was he sure, he said we can call it a wedding gift. I told him about what happened in our old house and he had his people to come build this. According to him it's a fortress so you can feel safe here and the kids can play outside without us worrying."

"Messiah." I repeated myself. "Oh my God."

"I know. Come on. Let's go check it out. I've been wanting to see the inside since I first came up here."

"Is it in our names?" I asked and he went in the glove compartment of his new Infiniti truck and passed me the deed that was indeed in both of our names. I was absolutely taken aback, and he hopped out to help me. Once I was sturdy on my walker, he grabbed the kids. They went from being knocked out sleep to running all over the grass in the front of the house. We laughed and shook our heads. I stood in the front, taking in the view and it was remarkable. The autumn blend travertine marble tile that they used for the road leading to our home and for the driveway was one of the most expensive tiles you could use, and it brought such a warm and inviting feeling to the premises. The interior designer in me was screaming over all of the small details I was peeping that I knew Messiah didn't even recognize but my eye was trained for it. I was beyond impressed already.

"Come on y'all." Messiah said and without a second thought they all came running. I would have had to call their little asses a million times. I rolled my eyes and

Sih laughed but that was cut short as the door opened. The ceilings had to be at least twenty feet and we were greeted by the most beautiful double staircase I've ever laid eyes on. The warm and inviting feeling that I felt upon driving up was the same feeling that came over me as we walked further into our new home.

It took over an hour and a golf cart ride to see the entire lay of the land. This was far more house than we actually needed, and I immediately knew that this wasn't just a wedding gift, this was also an apology gift. Mauricio is a good man and when you're in his presence you can feel it. I honestly believe he's extremely fucked up behind not knowing his other sons and being deprived of his right as a father. This home screamed "forgive me."

"We're never going to get them to leave that treehouse." We sat in the backyard watching the kids play. They needed this freedom after being cooped up in the hospital every day, so we chilled and allowed them to burn some energy.

"Not without kicking and screaming." We laughed. "You happy? Do you like it?"

"I love it baby. It's so new I can still kinda smell the paint. It's everything we wanted and so much more. You actually have a full fuckin' basketball court in there. Mauricio is insanely wealthy because this shit ain't normal." I slowly responded.

"Is it stupid of me not to want to accept this or at least give him his money back?" He kept his head straight as he stared up at the kids. "I just don't want him thinking he has to buy our love or no shit like that. In the beginning I didn't know how to feel about that nigga but now, I know it was my momma and I'm not really trippin'. Shit, ain't no sense in crying over spilled milk. He's apologized a million times for some shit that was out of his control. This house seems like another apology or obligation."

"No, it's not stupid, but I think you should have a talk with him and tell him he doesn't have to do things like this to gain your love or trust."

"We chopped it up, he knows."

"Then accept it, Baby. He's your father and he wants to do nice things for you, there's nothing wrong with that." He looked at me and smirked.

"I love you."

"I love you too, Handsome." I kissed him and then we both cuddled up to each other and watched the kids be kids.

****

Messiah said he didn't want any of the furniture from the old house and I agreed. This was a fresh start, so we needed everything to be fresh. The estate was fully furnished when we arrived, but we changed quite a few things to make it our own. Although we made several changes to the main house, we kept the guest house and the pool house the same. The guest house had two bedrooms and looked like a smaller version of the main house and I was still in awe every time I took the golf cart over there. It wasn't extremely far but it took about ten minutes if you're walking. We had five acres and every acre had something, whether it was the guest house, the tennis court, go kart track for the kids, and we had a beautiful canopy style shed off of the lake where Sih already had jet skis, canoes, and the cutest little paddle boats for the kids.

"Bitch, I can't even believe this house." Zionna had been over the last couple days and she kept saying the same shit over and over. "I think y'all should have y'all wedding here. As a matter of fact, we need some joy in our life and your wedding is going to do just that. We can't put a date to it until after Kabrina is back from rehab, we find Lyss, and lay Syd to rest, but we could and should at least start planning." I thought about what she said, and I couldn't have agreed more. I was ready to say I do to the man that stole my heart and chose never to give it back. We had a lot going on but none of it was going to hinder us from exchanging vows and committing ourselves to each other for eternity.

"Good idea. Let's go to the backyard and start brainstorming."

"Yay." She clapped and I smiled. I hadn't seen her this happy since Nash was killed. If this wedding was going to bring us all a happiness that we hadn't felt in quite a while, then this was definitely the right choice.

Messiah

Mauricio Vargas has been a man of his word since the day we met, and I fuck with that heavily. Not only did he have Fernando, but my grandfather Antonio, also had Toya as promised. The charges against Jaxsyn were as good as dropped now that we had her, and I couldn't have been happier. Unfortunately, Gato was still in the wind but I knew it was only a matter of time before we found him. Giz said he had gotten a couple camera hits on him, but nothing major. His time was coming though, we all knew it.

Antonio asked to meet with me, and I agreed. Like Mauricio, he came all this way to right some wrongs and I appreciated it. They jumped right into their roles as my father and grandfather, and I didn't fight them on it. I understood they didn't play a part in not being in me and Nash life and the only one to blame was my mother who had been MIA for weeks. She didn't have to do that though because I was done with her ass. Her absence was more telling than any excuse she could come up with.

"Nieto." He opened his arms and embraced me. "Have a seat." We were in his hotel suite and I could see that Vargas's don't do anything on a small scale. He had a presidential suite, and it was just him.

"How are you?" I asked as he sat down slowly.

"Old." He laughed at himself and I chuckled. "I called you here because I want to know you. We have to start somewhere and since I won't be staying much longer, I figured why not start now." He lit a cigar and passed me one. I wasn't big on cigars, but he started telling me how often they smoke cigars in Colombia and showed me how and what to look for. That sparked more conversations and before I knew it, I had spent the whole day with him. We talked about everything under the sun, smoked, drank, and ate good. He was by far one of the coolest men I had ever met and to know that he was my grandfather brought a sense of pride on. I really enjoyed him and right before I was about to leave, Carmine and Mauricio showed up. I had been avoiding Carmine, but Antonio addressed the elephant in the room before it could even become awkward or uncomfortable like it normally did.

"No one in this world can ever replace the bond you and Nashon had. When you speak on his name, I can feel the love that was shared." My father nodded his head as Antonio spoke. "Carmine is not a replacement Messiah, but he *is* your brother, and you can't ignore his presence forever. I won't sit back and allow you to miss out on forging a different kind of bond with him either, simply because you're in your head about something that you shouldn't be in your head about. I want you to try to embrace all of us because we've all been robbed. We're all victims to the lies and deceit that one person caused, and that person is not present so there should be no animosity here."

"He's right. I'm not trying to take our brother's place in your life, but I can't lie and say I don't want to start a relationship of my own with you. You're my little brother and you haven't said shit to me since the first day you said what up."

"My bad. All this shit is new to me. It's always just been me and Nash before my granny saved us. Shit, it took years for us to even trust our cousins because we had been let down so many times. When you've been through the shit I've been through, opening up is not that easy."

"Then let's take this shit slow but we gotta start somewhere."

"I got y'all." Carmine hugged me and I reciprocated his embrace. We all picked up right where me and Antonio left off and within no time, we were all laughing and joking. The shit actually felt good, and the day turned out to be perfect.

****

I agreed to allow my father to be the one that killed Fernando because their history dated back to before I was even thought of. Fernando had made my father's life hell since they were little kids and he deserved to get his revenge for all of Fernando's wrongdoing over the years, especially ordering the hits on him and having Jose to be the one to carry it out, but I needed to get mine too. This pussy ass nigga and his son has put my family through fuckin' hell and we still didn't know where the fuck Alyssa was. For that and the rest of the hoe shit they've done, I was going to make this bitch pay. I had Solo strip that nigga down to nothing and strap him down to a medical table. His arms were free but that was it. His feet were duct taped to the stirrups and the look of fear on his face brought me a great deal of pleasure.

"Fresh, roll those tanks in for me," I said as I thumped the needle in my hand. I walked closer to Fernando and smirked at how pale his skin had turned. I injected him with a Ketamine and Propofol mix that my brother and I used to inject muthafuckas with back in the day. The effects were immediate. He couldn't move his legs or arms, but he could still feel everything. The balance of the two drugs were extremely important because too much of one and not the other could put him to sleep and I wanted this bitch wide awake.

"He look like a hoe that's about to get fucked." Giz's crazy ass said as he came in with Fresh pushing one of the two tanks that had six baby piranhas swimming around. "This nigga need some pants on cuz. Shit got me

189

feeling uncomfortable as fuck." We all died laughing at this fool because he was dead ass serious.

"Nah. He good just like he is. This nigga thought he could fuck us over and that's exactly what his karma is going to be." I raised one of his arms and that bitch fell like a noodle. He was ready. I had them to put both of his arms in the tanks with the piranhas and he started screaming. They didn't waste no time chewing on that nigga. "Where the fuck is Alyssa?" I grabbed the lightening rod style tasers and stuck that bitch right on his nuts. Every nigga in the room cringed knowing how bad that shit hurt. I lit his ass up and he was yelling and screaming but he still wasn't telling me what I wanted to hear so I alternated between his dick, balls, and asshole. Tears poured from his eyes as he laid there unable to move but feeling all seven million volts of electricity that I sent surging through his lower half as the piranhas nibbled at his now open wounds on his arms. The water in the tank was already pink from his blood and they were just getting started and so was I. "Where the fuck is Alyssa, Fernando?" I slapped him hard as fuck with the taser and then stuck that bitch on his neck. He passed out and we woke his bitch ass right back up. Wasn't no sleep happening on my watch. I lit the taser and stuck on his "gooch" area without letting up.

"Okay, okay, okay," he said breathlessly. His once pale skin was now beet red. He had shit and pissed himself and probably realized there was no escaping this so he could either die with the information or give it up and play with his odds. He still hadn't seen Mauricio so he probably thought he had a chance of making it but that wasn't even an option. "She's in Gato's playhouse. I know he's not there because he's gone rogue and he's avoiding places I would look for him, and that's one of them. I'll give you the address, please just stop. I'm begging you." We got the address and I still put another two hours in on torturing his ass. He deserved more but when he passed out the last time,

I let him stay out. I had to go find my little sister, but I wasn't finished with his ass. He's going to feel the pain we've felt for months because of the orders he put into motion.

This was just the beginning, then I'm passing him off to his brother.

Alyssa

I was lying in the middle of the floor hungry and lethargic. I had no energy, and my body was cramping all over. The hard floor had finally taken its toll on my body and my baby. There were no parts of my body that wasn't being affected by my sleeping conditions, lack of food, and literally no water. The random girl that helped me hadn't been in here in a couple days and the last time she came she literally had one pack of crackers like you get from restaurants and she said there was no water. I cried as I dried my mouth out even more trying to swallow saltines with nothing to chase it with. I was a horrible mother already and it killed me that I couldn't give my baby the proper nutrition that he or she deserved.

Although Gato hadn't been messing with me lately, I still was on edge every second of everyday. I still wake up in a different colored room every day, but he hadn't put anything in the room in about a week. It had to be that amount of time or close to it. Last thing he did was put so many frogs in the room I couldn't even move. Well I couldn't move because they were everywhere but also because when I woke up I had cuts all over the bottom of my feet. I could barely stand, and they hopped all night, so eventually I moved them to the side and curled up in the corner. I woke up in a royal blue room with hundreds of black and white hypnotic circles on the wall. Looking at them made me dizzy as hell so I just laid in the middle of the floor praying that he wouldn't dump some random animal or insect on me again. He was legit crazy.

If he was watching me, I didn't have to do much pretending that I was being broken down because his mind games were definitely working. I was at my lowest point ever and I didn't know how much longer I could go on. My prayers had long ago fallen on deaf ears because I knew at this point, help wasn't coming. I was alone and there was no telling how long he would play these games with me until he got tired and finished me off. He was already starving me and that in itself could have been part of his games. Who knows really? This guy was certifiably insane and unpredictable.

The door to the room I was being held in unlocked and I didn't even have the energy to lift my head. All I could do was hope that it was the one girl and this time she had water for me. I couldn't even imagine going another day without at least a sip. My lips were so dry they were cracking.

"Come on, I got you sis." I heard Messiah's voice and belted out the hardest deepest cry that I could muster up. Never in a million years did I imagine when I heard that door unlock that my brother would be the one walking in.

"Sih." I buried my head in his chest because I actually couldn't believe that he saved me. I had prayed so hard for him to find me and just when I lost hope, he came through.

"I know baby girl. You're safe now." I held on to him so tight I damn near cut off both of our circulation. "Aye, make sure y'all free all of them. Check every room, this crazy ass nigga got women and kids tied up all around this bitch." Messiah yelled behind him as we made our way out outside. I couldn't stop trembling even though I knew I was safe. I also wouldn't let him go so he had someone to drive us wherever we were going as I cried in his arms. I wanted to ask about my sister, but I couldn't take hearing that she didn't give a fuck about my well-being right now. I wasn't mentally strong enough to deal with her rejection, so I kept quiet and tried my best to control my emotions.

My eyes fluttered open and I thought Gato was playing tricks on me again until I realized that I had a needle in my arm, monitors hooked to me, and Jax and Zionna were sleep holding my hands.

"Hi TT." I looked across the room and burst into an uncontrollable fit of tears. Nevaeh was rocking her baby doll and smiling at me.

"Hi baby. TT Lyssa missed you so much."

"You miss me TT?" Jeniah said from the other side of Jax. I hadn't seen her, but she was reaching for me. I reached my arms out and it woke Jax and Z since they were holding my hands.

"No Niah, TT is sick." Zionna said causing Jeniah to fold her arms and pout.

"It's okay." I opened my arms again and she climbed in bed with me and put her back to Zionna causing us all to laugh.

"How do you feel?" Jax asked slowly and her voice was slightly different, but I was too nervous to address it or even look her way. Last time we spoke she was so mean that I didn't want to upset her and go through that again. I avoided eye contract and told her I was okay.

"Destiny." Zionna called out and a beautiful black woman who was dressed like she had just stepped off of a magazine cover for the rich and famous appeared. "Do you mind taking the kids for a moment so Jax and I can speak to our little sister?"

"I don't mind at all. Come on sweet babies. Let's go do our nails while your brother naps," she said, and I gasped because they'd gotten Junior back. Z smiled and squeezed my hand knowing that the news of our nephew being back was everything to me.

"You've missed a lot, love. Umm," She paused and looked at Jaxsyn whose eyes were filled with tears. Something happened and I could feel it. "Umm, the day Gato or his people kidnapped you, Jax and Sih went to get

194

Junior. They found him and Kabrina and as they were leaving, Gato started shooting at them from a helicopter." My heart started racing thinking about what my family had been through. This shit was all too much and for what? "Umm he," her words trailed off and both her and Jax had tears streaming down their faces. I sat all the way up as my chest tightened. Jax has been more than my sister, she's been my best friend my whole life and I've only saw her this hurt less than a hand full of times. I was so nervous about what Z was about to tell me. "He uhh, dropped something in front of their car causing Sih to swerve and hit a pole. Jax and Junior went flying through the windshield. We later found out that it was Sydnee that he dropped from the helicopter." Jax dropped her head, and I didn't know what to say. I waited for Zionna to continue but she just kept crying.

"And then what happened? Was it way up in the air? Will she ever walk again?"

"No baby," Jax was still talking the same and then I realized her head was wrapped and she had a walker on the side of her. I started trembling as I stared at her. "she didn't... make... it... Lyss." Nothing in this world could have prepared me for the instant pain that shot through my body. My voice was caught in my throat for a full minute before I screamed out in sheer agony. Not my fucking little sister. My world was officially shattered.

Mauricio

As my driver drove me to where Fernando was being kept, I couldn't help thinking about how bad I wanted this shit to be over. When Carmine called to tell me the plan worked, and that they had him, I became anxious and almost excited. Now that a few days has passed, I'm just ready for my son to have his life back and get back to living mine. Twenty years of bullshit and two of our sons lost, over jealousy and greed was far too much and it was all because I allowed my brother to slide one too many times. Those days were over. I couldn't allow him to make it this time. He took my oldest son from me and turned my youngest son's life upside down. Shit, his ass had me shot twice and left for dead. I couldn't allow him to breathe another day.

"Hello." I answered my phone for Destiny.

"I miss you." I knew that tone anywhere and it made me smile.

"I miss you too, baby. I'll be back at the hotel soon."

"I'll wait up for you."

"Naked?" I asked and she giggled.

"What other way is there?"

"That's my baby. How were things at the estate?"

She sighed. "Jaxsyn's sister is better today than she was yesterday but they can't get her blood pressure down and that's dangerous for the baby she's carrying."

"She's pregnant? I didn't know that."

"Yeah, a couple months, I think. It's so sad baby. Your brother has done a number on them and they all seem like really great people."

"I know." Was all I said because that was exactly what I needed to hear before walking into the place that I would kill the only brother I have left. "I have to go Baby, but I'll see you soon."

"I love you, Mauricio."

"I love you more, Baby." I disconnected the call and stepped out. Messiah's truck was parked outside, along with a few motorcycles. I texted him and let him know I was here and by the time I made it to the door, Solo was opening it.

"What up doe?" He spoke.

"Hey, he still breathing?" I joked because I knew Messiah wanted nothing more than to kill his ass, but I'll let him handle my nephew, Fernando needed to die by my hand.

"Hell yeah. Evil doesn't die that easily. Prez torturing the fuck out of him, but nothing that's going to kill his ass. Shit is genius if you ask me."

We walked all the way to the back, and I wanted to laugh at the sight before me. My son was damn sure at his wits end. He had my brother strapped to a damn hospital table in stirrups, and had his bitch lying face down over some kind of plastic container that had snakes in it. They were biting the shit out of her, puncturing different parts of her with each bite. He had the bitch Toya and her grandmother hanging upside down like bats, and four bodies that I didn't recognize were off to the side getting cut up by his people and dropped into acid. Lace was probably one of the bodies because I knew my father had handled her immediately after finding out she was snake.

"This is a sight to see." My father walked up to me and I nodded. "Funny how that Vargas blood works. We weren't even in his life but he's just like us." We watched my son sit back in his chair as he tased the shit out of Fernando. To the naked eye this was gruesome and would make most think he was crazy or sadistic, but to me, someone that's lived this life for a long ass time, I was proud. These muthafuckas turned his whole life upside down and this is what they all deserved.

"Fernando know you here yet?"

"No. I've been back here watching my grandson work. This is day number three. He's done all kinds of shit to him and now he's back to tasing him which seems to be the most painful."

"Let's go show my dear brother what a couple of ghosts look like." I started walking because I couldn't wait any longer. I've waited for this moment for years.

Messiah looked back over his shoulder as he smoked a blunt and gave us a head nod. We nodded back as he turned back around and tased Fernando's ball sack. You could tell he was winded and damn near out of it but as soon as those volts hit him, his ass came to life and howled out in sheer agony. His pain brought me pleasure and I slowly walked up closer.

"Hello, brother." I spoke with a smirk on my face and Messiah hopped up.

"You nasty muthafucka!" We all busted out laughing. Fernando shit himself and the look of disgust on my son's face was priceless. Fernando was well aware that it was over at this point. He'd proved time and time again that this world wasn't big enough for the both of us and I was going to make sure he got his wish. Unfortunately for him, his demise would correct this issue and not mine.

"Son, it didn't have to be this way." Fernando's eyes popped open, and he went back and forth between the two of us. See, when Jose shot me, people didn't know whether I was dead or alive including our father. He confronted Jose and Fernando and they both lied, but they knew that he was on to them. What did they do? Ordered a hit on their own father but when you're as respected as our father, shit like that doesn't just happen without it getting around to that person, which it did.

I remember lying in the hospital bed in sheer disbelief that not only would they shoot me, but also attempt to kill our father. Fernando embodied evil and for some reason Jose followed his lead. I could tell my dad was hurt as fuck, but he did what anyone in his position would do, he paid the person that was paid to do the job and he went back and told my brothers that my father was dead. They actually threw a party that night and my father sat in his car watching them celebrate his death. Something changed in him that night and it made my hate for my brothers deepen.

Later that night my father killed the guy that brought the information to him simply because he was a loose end, and then went back to Colombia. His street dealings were done so there was no way Fernando and Jose would know he was still alive, and they hadn't even reached out to our mother for funeral details or anything. Seeing my parents hurt like that was hard but this bitch was going to pay for all that shit today.

"I thought..." His head dropped backwards, and Messiah slapped his ass so hard the wand of the taser almost broke in half.

"Wake the fuck up!"

"Thought I was dead? You didn't have enough money or respect to carry that out." He walked over to him and whispered something in his ear. Fernando's facial expression was that of shock and awe and then anger. Without anything else being said, my father walked right out the door.

"I'm out too. I'm over these muthafuckas." Messiah pulled his Glock off of his waist and lit Toya and her grandmother asses up causing Rebecca to scream and cry out for help. "Man, shut the fuck up. Was yo' ass doing all that fuckin' hollering when my girl was trusting you with our business and you were running back to this grimy muthafucka? Where was this energy when this muthafucka put a hit out on me and my brother? Fuck out of here with that stupid shit. Aye, put this bitch arms in the tank and add the rest of the snakes to this pit. She obviously worried about the wrong shit, so we need to apply more pressure." He walked out and his men started doing what he told them to do.

"Looks like it's just us, brother."

"Fuck you."

I nodded and grabbed the machete off of the table of tools that Messiah had laid out. There were no words that needed to be spoken on my part. I simply started slicing. I needed to get back to the hotel to make love to my naked wife. Nothing I said to Fernando was going to change what he'd done to me and my family so there was no point in going back and forth. I made every slit to his skin count and made sure he felt the years of pain that he inflicted on others.

"That's for Nashon," I said, staring him right in his eyes as he took his last breath from the machete piercing his heart.

Messiah

"Sssss." Jax hissed as I laid between her thighs feasting on her middle. I missed the way she tasted, her touch, her warmth, and just being us. We used to wake up on one every day and lately we had been so obsessed with everything going on around us that we hadn't had any time to just enjoy each other. I decided to change that, and I woke her up how I used to, with my face between her legs and she immediately started grinding and winding her hips. Shit had me hard as a rock and I couldn't wait to slide inside of her. "Fuck!" Her back arched and she balled the sheets up in her hands as her body drenched me and I swear that shit was heaven on earth. I kept suckin' until she gave it to me again and again. Next thing I knew, her ass was snoring. I couldn't do shit but laugh. I needed to hop in the shower anyway and get my day started so I wasn't even tripping even though a nigga was definitely hard as fuck.

After I got dressed, I went downstairs, and Alyssa was sitting at the table staring down at her new phone I'd bought her. She was so occupied that she hadn't even heard me come in. This wasn't anything new from her. Since she's been back, she hasn't been the same. Hell, it's almost been a week and yesterday was her first day coming out of the room, and she only came out because she wanted to see the kids, and no one had brought them to her. Other than that, her ass would have been in her room crying like she did every day.

"You good, sis?" She jumped and damn near fell out of her chair.

"Jesus, Sih. Why would you sneak up on me like that?"

"I been in the kitchen a good five minutes, Baby Girl." I waved my juice that I had grabbed from the refrigerator and she smiled.

"Sorry. Yeah, I'm good."

"You sure? You don't look good." I sat down across from her."

"Kevin…" She sighed and rolled her eyes.

"Dr. Messer? What about him? I gotta beat his ass? I got a lot going on right now, but I can make time."

She smiled and shook her head. "No." She started telling me what happened the day she was snatched up and I was genuinely surprised. Alyssa is a sweetheart and she put that nigga all the way on blast, but I was also proud of her because he was on some fuck nigga shit. Now his wife is really leaving him and he's telling Alyssa that he's not mad and wants to work shit out. Nah… fuck that. As a man and her brother, I kept that shit real and let her know that she was the second choice. That means when his wife calms down, he'll either go back if she allows him, hit if she allows it, or Lyss will become the main and he'll find someone else to fill her spot on the side. At this point, all his ass needed to do was take care of their kid and get the fuck from around my little sister.

She cried and then agreed that their shit was a wrap. We kicked it for about an hour as I schooled her on real men and then she told me how hurt she was over Syd. I knew her pain firsthand and told her it was okay to mourn her sister, but it wasn't okay to stay in mourning. Something I also knew from experience. I told her to talk to Z too. She said she would, then went upstairs to hideaway again.

Just as I was about to slide out, my phone alerted me that someone was at the gate. I looked at the cameras and it was Carmine. Ever since we all chilled with Antonio, he's been hittin' me up and coming around more. He wasn't forcing himself on me but he damn sure was inserting himself into my life.

I buzzed him in and a few minutes later he was walking into the kitchen. "Aye Jax gon' let you keep the housekeeper? That bitch bad as fuck."

"Bad? You crazy as hell. Basic at most."

"Basic? Get the fuck outta here. I'll bend that ass over in a heartbeat."

"I mean she's fuckable but nah, compared to what I have upstairs, she ain't even worth a second glance."

"Well shit, when you put it like that." We both busted out laughing.

"Oh Sih, can you get my dress from the cleaners for the funeral. Daddy put it in there yesterday. I would ask him but he's still upstairs sleeping."

"I got you." I told Lyss, and she went to walk away but Carmine spoke up.

"Obviously my little brother is rude. I'm Carmine, what's your name Snow?"

"Alyssa, his sister and please don't call me Snow, especially since you're just as white as me."

"Correction, you're white, I'm a beautifully melanated King, Mami." We all laughed, and I shook my head. Him and Nash would have fuckin' loved each other.

"Whatever."

"*Whatever.*" He mocked her and she gave him a deep ass side eye that I know she got from Jaxsyn because I've gotten that look a few times. "I'm fuckin' with you, Beautiful, you gon' let me call you sometime?"

"Hell no. I'm pregnant and confused." I died fuckin' laughing and so did she. It was no lies told about that, but the way she said it was hilarious.

"Let me bring some clarity to your world." He got up and took her phone out of her hand and put his number in and then called his phone to have her number. She shook her head and then walked away. "That's your future sister-in-law."

"She's that anyway. That's Jax's lil sister."

"Blood?"

"Yeah." I chuckled. "Same daddy different momma. The bitch that's laying on top of them snakes back at the warehouse is her mom."

"Get the fuck out of here." I went all the way back to the beginning and brought him up to speed on everything. Coming out here, all he knew is that he had a brother from a woman that Mauricio didn't cheat on his mother with, and Fernando and Gato was fuckin' with me. He said our father kept it real short and to the point. I broke that shit all the way down and he was speechless, which I'm learning is rare for this nigga. "Damn, man. I know that fucked your girl's head up big time."

"You have no idea." I passed him a juice from the refrigerator, and we chopped it up until the kids came running in and I started making breakfast. The sound of all three of my babies giggling brought me the joy I've needed since the day I laid them down for a nap and our world got flipped upside down. They played with Carmine and then Jaxsyn and Z came in and started helping me cook. Jax grabbed the bread to make French toast while Z turned on the music just as I got another alert for the gate. It was Mauricio and Destiny, so I buzzed them in. Destiny was in love with Jax, Z, and the kids. We didn't talk too much, and I figured that had everything to do with me being an outside child so I didn't trip. She was never rude, she just didn't fuck with me.

"Pass me the orange juice, Jax. Alyssa, come eat!" Zionna called out and Jax passed her the juice. "Just Alyssa?" Jagger asked and pushed Zionna playfully as he looked down at the spread.

"Shut up, punk. I thought you and Meka left last night.

"Jaxsyn made us stay because it was late. She'll be down in a minute. This looks really good."

"Thanks, but Sih did most of it."

"I do what I can, when I can." I joked and we all laughed as everyone started making their way into the kitchen. I pulled Jaxsyn to the side and she stared up at me with nothing but love in her eyes. I hadn't seen that sparkle in so long that I couldn't do shit but smile and then kiss her pretty ass. "Look." I turned her around and wrapped my arms around her. We watched our family move around the kitchen making plates, dancing to the music, joking around, and playing with the kids. We still had a lot of shit going on, but today felt different. Today felt normal, and we hadn't had a glimpse of normal in so long that I wanted us to appreciate this moment while we were in it. We deserved every day to be like this and today was the start of the happiness I promised my baby in the beginning. I didn't give a fuck about Gato being on the loose. He'll be handled eventually. This moment and moments just like it was what was most important to me and what I needed to focus my attention on.

"My heart is full, Baby." Her words came out clear, and I kissed her head. She was talking so much better these days. She was definitely still working on her speech, but the difference was obvious.

"Mine too, Tink."

"Mommy," Jeniah called Jax and then started going off, but she was talking so fast trying to tell on Carmine that her words were jumbled. My baby was going to say what she had to say regardless, and we all roared with laughter. She was going to be our hot head and she get that shit honest. She had us damn near in tears with her gibberish and looking at everybody like "this shit ain't funny."

"What else baby?" Jax asked and Niah continued on her rant pointing at Carmine and all we could make out was

"Untle" instead of uncle, making it funnier. Even though Sydnee's funeral is tomorrow, this was the morale boost that we all definitely needed, without even knowing how badly we needed it. I couldn't speak for anyone else, but I thanked God for this moment. It was a long time coming...

Jaxsyn

Sydnee looked like sleeping beauty and it made saying goodbye to my baby sister even harder. This day was one of the worst of my life but thank God for Messiah Mauricio Knight. My baby had his hand in every aspect of the day and looked out for me and my entire family. My daddy lost his shit when they started lowering Syd into the ground and Sih was right there to catch him. He held my dad in his arms as he cried hysterically. There was no toxic masculinity or ego present, just love and understanding. I couldn't have asked for a better man to share my life with, and he proved that shit every single day.

After the repast everyone except Alyssa went their separate ways. Alyssa didn't want to leave my side and I would never force her to. She was still very jumpy, and I think more than wanting to be with her big sister, she wanted to be near Messiah. She felt safe around him and we were both okay with her staying with us as long as she needed to. There was plenty of room and the kids loved having TT Lyss around.

"I want to thank you." I walked into our closet where Messiah was undressing. I kissed his back and he looked over his shoulder at me.

"What you got to thank me for Tink?" He turned around wrapping me in his warm embrace. I swear there was no place I ever wanted to be. His security and love were everything to me and I nestled into him. Before I spoke, I took a moment to listen to his heart beat. It was my favorite sound other than our children's laughter. He stroked my head already knowing what I was doing.

"For being you. I know being in the same cemetery as Nash today was hard, but you pushed your own feelings to the side to be there for me and my family. When Dawson lost control at the funeral, you were right there to hold him up and before my daddy could do something stupid when they started lowering Syd into the ground, you caught him and allowed him to break down in your arms too. No ego, no toxic masculinity, just men with a shared pain. My sisters know when you're near, they're safe, and I appreciate you for opening yourself up to them and making yourself available for us all to love you. You're perfection in my eyes Messiah, and I know you hate when I say that, but you are, and I love and appreciate you more than you'll ever know." I started kissing his chest.

Today I buried my little sister, and it was hands down one of the lowest moments of my life, but today also revealed more of the man I planned to marry. I watched Sih run around like a chicken with its head cut off making sure that everyone from my father on down was good and at one point I couldn't take my eyes off of him. I couldn't get over how blessed I was. Of all the women that has thrown themselves at him over the years, he chose me. He didn't just choose me based on looks or sexual desire, he chose me the first day he laid eyes on me because even from a distance, he knew I was for him. He didn't care about my situation or the fact that I turned him down repeatedly. Messiah knew in his soul that I was his and what he wanted from me. He stayed diligent until I realized what he had known from the very start.

"You know what I love and appreciate, Tink?" He pulled away, making me look up at him. "Your heart. We buried your little sister today and instead of you dwelling on the sadness and darkness that comes along with a loss of this caliber, you're standing in front of me singing my praises. Praises I don't even deserve." He picked me up and sat me on the table that was in the middle of our closest. "I appreciate how selfless you are. I appreciate the mother that you are. I appreciate the woman you are and the wife you're going to be. Today I did what needed to be done so there's no need to thank me, but I love that with everything going on you took the time out to say what you just said." He kissed me and then took my bottom lip into his mouth. I moaned and he smirked. "I appreciate your hard work and dedication to getting better. You barely even paused just now Beautiful. When you came out of that coma, they said your recovery was unpredictable because when dealing with the brain, things can get tricky, and you said *tricky my ass*." We both laughed. "You didn't let up baby and you fought through this shit like a trooper. No matter how frustrated you became, I never heard you complain once." He started kissing on my neck. "You inspire me to be better and do better, so when you see me doing shit that seems perfect, I took my cues from you." *Shit.*

My body was on fire and I yearned for him to make love to me. With all the bullshit happening in our life, sex and intimacy took a backseat but we had our children back now, most of our enemies were taking dirt naps, we had a brand-new home, and our life was getting back on track. It was okay for us to relax a little and just enjoy each other for a moment.

I ran my fingers through his braids and caressed the back of his neck. His hands stroked the sides of my body sending chills rippling all over me. He hungrily kissed me, and I yearned for more. We needed this. I slid off of the table and tugged at his briefs. Dropping to my knees I looked up and couldn't help but to lick my lips. His fuckin' body was sick and the way he was staring down at me had me leaking.

My chin was wet from giving him the nastiest head he probably ever received in his life, but he was warned. I told him, once this ring was on my finger this was going to be his usual.

"Got damn Jaxsyn." He planted his feet and continued staring down at me in amazement as I looked up at him. I used both hands to twist up and down his shaft as I sucked on his head. I switched up on him and started deep throating him which took me forever to perfect, but his reaction let me know he was grateful for the time I put into learning how to thoroughly please him.

Forty-five minutes of head had him weak as fuck. Every time he grabbed my head and thought he was about to cum I pulled back. I wanted to make love to him with my mouth and really show him how much he was loved. He's been my rock since the very beginning and more than ever for the last few months, I wanted him to feel every bit of my appreciation.

"Fuuuck!" He groaned out as I sucked his balls into my mouth with ease and continued to stroke his dick. I wasn't playing any games. I continued down a little further and licked his gooch area. That very sensitive area between his balls and his ass. This was a first and when his head went back, and he gripped the table so hard I could hear his knuckles cracking, I knew those bitches on Pornhub hadn't let me down. Two seconds later I was deep throating him again and he was releasing down my throat. No words were spoken as he emptied himself. He was stuck and his body was stiff as a board. I kept suckin' and he never got soft.

He picked me up and stared at me with pure love dancing in his brown orbs. This shit was forever and couldn't nobody tell me otherwise.

"Siiiih." I purred as he slid me down his shaft.

"Why you so wet Tink?" He whispered against my neck sensually. "Pleasing me got you dripping like this Ma?"

"Yessss. I love pleasing my man." I moaned as he hit my spot, purposely making me shudder.

"Oh yeah?" He started deep stroking me and the tables had turned just that quickly.

"Yeeeah." I tossed my head back as tears rolled down my face. His methodic strokes had me stuck and begging him for more and to stop at the same time. My deepest inner region felt like it shifted from the lashing Messiah was giving me. We hadn't gotten down like this since the very beginning.

"I fuckin' love yo' ass so much Ma." He was staring at me intensely with his bottom lip folded under his perfect teeth and I started squirting all over him. His ass was too sexy, and the strokes were hitting too right for me not to. "Shit baby." He smirked. I was drenching his ass and with every shot to my gut came a shower. I couldn't stop and once his ego was involved, he damn sure wasn't about to let up.

"Ahhhh." I cried out. "I love you too Daddy. Shit, I love you so much." I was trying to match his rhythm but there was no matching tonight. He was in savage mode and before I knew it, we were both bellowing out inaudible pleasure and I fell straight into a much-needed slumber.

****

Something was different about Zionna and since we were getting together to go over my wedding plans, I was going to address it. She seemed happier but very distracted and because we've had so much going on I felt like we needed to reconnect. We hadn't talked about where she was mentally over what happened with Sandy, we hadn't gone into detail over what was happening with her and Fresh, we hadn't even discussed her staying or going back to AZ. We hadn't really talked at all, and before I fail at this sister shit again, I needed her to check in with me.

"You sure you don't want to come downstairs? It's just me and Z."

"Sure." Alyssa scooted out of bed and I smiled.

"I still can't believe you're about to have a baby." I rubbed her little pudge. "My baby is having a baby."

"I can't believe it either." She shook her head with a grin as we made our way downstairs. Zionna got up from the table when she saw us, and we all hugged. Our relationship with each other was solid. Z is over every other day checking on us and we do the same for her. Shit, the only time Alyssa's left her room was when Carmine forced her, anything dealing with the kids, or if she's going to visit Zionna. The last couple weeks things had really normalized in our circle. It almost felt too good to be true, but Sih assured me that even though Gato was still loose we had nothing to worry about, so I didn't.

"Z are you staying out here or going back to Arizona so I can wrap my head around it because now I'm attached, and I don't wanna see you go?" Alyssa said and I was happy she did since it was on my list of things I needed to talk to Zionna about.

"Y'all, I don't know." She started blushing. "Fresh and I have been getting closer and he's willing to stay in Detroit if I am."

"Closer?" Both Lyss and I said at the same time.

"Yeah. Close then closer." Her smile could have lit up the city it was so bright. "I haven't felt this good since Nash and I hate to say that because they're cousins, but I haven't. I feel like I'm in such a perfect space in my life right now. I'm healing every day, I haven't had one drink in weeks, I sleep at night without having nightmares, I can think about Nash and be happy about what we shared instead of our memories sending me into a self-destructive spiral. I can honestly smile from genuine happiness instead of smiling through my hidden pain."

"Oh wooow. I'm loving what I see already. I'm here for it sis." Alyssa was smiling from ear to ear and so was I. She was glowing and it was a good look.

"Me too." I agreed and Z looked at me.

"Really? I thought you would feel some kind of way like Sih. He still hasn't spoken to me since the funeral.

I saw how he looked at me when I left here with Fresh that day and I really feel bad, but I can't deny myself happiness because it makes him uncomfortable," she said with her voice shifting from how giddy it was to a sadness over Sih's disapproval.

"Sih can't imagine betraying or being disloyal to his brother and once he realizes that he's not, he'll accept you two. Until then, ignore him and enjoy Fresh." I hugged her tight and she wiped the couple of tears that slid down her face.

"Whew. Anyway, what's up with you and Carmine?" We both looked at a smiling Alyssa.

"I don't know. I'm pregnant by another man and I'm still trying to navigate through my emotions about several things. Sih suggested that I leave Kevin alone, so I just talked to him about co-parenting and putting an end to everything else. Which he agreed was best as well. Since I'm just getting out of something, I don't think it's smart to start something else, plus my head is a mess right now."

"Well, he seems more than willing to stick around and help you navigate, Honey. I would see where it goes. If we haven't learned shit else within the last couple years, we've all learned that life is short. Don't dwell on shit that's out of your control sis."

"I agree." I nodded and Alyssa took a deep breath.

"Yeah. I agree too." She picked her phone up and we all hopped out of our feelings and started diving into wedding plans. I couldn't believe I was actually getting married again but this time was nothing like the first time. Black and I got married when I told him I was pregnant and after the vows were recited, he told me he wanted me to get an abortion. This time was the real deal, and I was going to finally get my forever.

"What's good y'all." Sih sexy ass walked into the kitchen with Carmine and Gizmo.

"Hey y'all." Fresh and Solo walked in right behind them. We all spoke and Sih started nibbling on my lips. We couldn't get enough of each other these days. We've always been sexually attracted to each other, but something changed between us and everything that we felt was heightened.

"Let me talk to you real quick." He grabbed my hand, and I was ready to drop it like it's hot until I realized that Solo was following us. I rolled my eyes so they couldn't see and once we were in the next room, I asked what was going on.

"Rebecca is a loose end that we need to tie up baby. What you wanna do? Personally, I don't want you getting your hands dirty, but I know her betrayal hit you deep."

"I hate her for everything she's put us through and cost us, but I'm over all of this bullshit. Solo I want her buried alive. Put the snakes in there with her and allow that hoe to die slow and painfully. Is Lace still alive?"

"Prez done rubbed off on you First Lady." Solo smirked and Sih shook his head. "Lace is a done deal. We got everyone but Gato and he's next."

"Give us a minute." Messiah said and Solo walked away. "He's going to be found so I don't want you worrying about shit but our wedding."

"I'm not worried at all." I wrapped my arms around him, and he kissed my head. "I need you to take it easy on Z. She's really happy again Sih. Nash is gone baby and she's not cheating on him. I know it may not be ideal for her and Fresh to go forward, but they're not trying to spit on Nash memory or be disrespectful in anyway. They just found solace in each other and after everything we've all been through, that should be a good thing. Right?"

He stared at me and shook his head. "I already talked to that nigga a couple days ago. They're grown, and it is what it is. Shit makes me uncomfortable, but I'll eventually get there."

I couldn't help but to smile and he started tickling me and telling me to chill out. I knew he would come around sooner or later, and he may still have a long way to go but I loved that he wasn't as angry as he was before. This was growth. We went back to the kitchen and everybody was boo'd up except Solo. Gizmo was standing by the sink chopping it up with our maid Alexa. I was surprised, but at the same time, she's a cute girl so I could see the attraction.

"I think we're all going to be okay, baby." I looked up at Sih.

"Without a doubt, Tink." He kissed me and we joined everybody for an impromptu game night. We called our usuals and told them to come over too. My daddy couldn't make it because he had an early flight to California to go see my momma but everyone else showed up and the night turned out to be a movie.

Finally, we were back to living, and it felt damn good.

One Year Later…

Jaxsyn

I was out with a few of the women who work for me, a couple friends, and my sisters for my bachelorette party that they went above and beyond for. We had taken a party bus over to Canada and partied hard, then came back to Detroit and continued the party with strippers, both male and female. We had MGM's hotel rockin' and because Sih's name carried weight in the city no one said shit to us. Well, we had every room on the floor occupied too so that may have made a difference.

I was having the time of my life and then I got a call from Gizmo and when my bro hits my line, I'll always stop whatever I'm doing and run to him which is exactly what I did.

"It sounded urgent," I said as I walked over to him. He was at one of Sih's warehouses.

"It is." He smirked. "I just got back in town last night, but I couldn't wait to give you your wedding gift. Real spit Jax, you're one of the dopest females I've ever fuckin' met and cuz is lucky as fuck to have you. I tell that nigga that shit all the time and his weak ass get to smiling and shit but I mean it every time I say it. I'll do anything for y'all asses, and I hope y'all know that."

"Vice versa. Nigga you saved my life and sanity more times than once. We can never repay you for all you've done for us, but I hope you know we appreciate you." I spoke directly from my heart and he nodded.

"Come on so I can give you your gift. You know I don't be fuckin' with this sap ass shit." He stood up and I busted out laughing. This nigga was tough as nails and when he felt his emotions rising, he suppressed the fuck out of them. Well, I'm sure he doesn't suppress them when he's around Alexa, who he brought back to New York with him. They live together now and according to Sih this nigga Giz was thinking about getting out of the streets and marrying her. I wasn't going to put him on blast, but I was proud of him.

We walked to the back and when he turned the lights on, I gasped from sheer disbelief as he smiled from ear to ear. "I told you, you my muhfucka and I meant that shit. Anyone who brings harm your way is a dead ass nigga." He had Gato strung up and stretched out into an X. I couldn't believe my eyes. As happy as I was and as good as life was, he was still in the back of my mind haunting my thoughts. I hated that he hadn't been caught, but here he was, in the flesh. "Happy Wedding Eve!"

"You so damn crazy." I laughed and hugged him tightly. He knew me so well. "There will never be another you. Blood couldn't make this bond stronger."

"On God." He kissed my head and passed me the Glock off his waist. "Wake yo' hoe ass up." Giz took a wooden paddle and slapped it across Gato's chest so hard it echoed throughout the warehouse and turned his skin red immediately. He tried to scream but it barely came out. His lips were crusty, so his throat was obviously dry as hell.

"One question and then I'm putting you out of your misery." I walked closer to him. "Why my little sister? I know why you did everything else. As sick and stupid the reason, I get it the logic behind it. She didn't do shit to you though, and she wasn't directly connected to Sih or Mauricio. She didn't deserve that shit and if you were trying to get back at Rebecca, why couldn't you just focus on her? That bitch deserved to get dropped from a helicopter, my little sister didn't."

"What's my name?" His voice came out in a whisper.

"What?"

"What's my name?"

"Nigga this ain't the time to be a smart ass." Gizmo said in a frustrated tone and I felt the same way.

"Fuck you. What's my name?"

I stuck my arm out just as Giz was about to head over to him. "Dominic."

He smiled. "Nah, my full name. Dominic Sidney Vargas. Her mother named her after her father. Rebecca's sick ass started fuckin' me when I was eleven years old. I thought I was in love with her because she played on my young mind. We used to fuck every damn day. She would even pick me up from school early so we wouldn't have to hide, and she could have her way with me. Years later when she got pregnant by me, she knew she would go to jail or my father would kill her ass, so she lied. The obvious choice was to say it was Brian's baby, but Sydnee was mine.

As I got older, I started realizing Rebecca wasn't shit but I knew she loved me and I loved her sick ass too. It was twisted because although I knew she was wrong, I was hooked by then. Sadly, I didn't know what to do with those newfound emotions and started lashing out in the streets. That's when *Gato* was born. The woman I loved and the mother of my child, was married and fuckin' my father. I had a lot of aggression and when she played me, and told y'all where your son was, I wanted to hurt her as bad as she'd hurt me. I was loyal to her ass my whole life. I could have told my father that she was suckin' my dick every time he wasn't around, but I loved her too much.

Meanwhile, she kept showing me that I wasn't shit to her, kept showing me that other people were more important.

Her snitching to Messiah was the last straw. It was my turn to show her disloyal ass just how it felt for a muthafucka to play you. I had a plan for all of you that was going to crush her soul, I just started with Alyssa and Sydnee. I had no intentions of dropping her when I started shooting at your car, but the more I looked at her and she looked just like her mother, I couldn't help but to let her--" I emptied the clip into him silencing him forever. I turned around and Giz was waiting for me with open arms. I broke the fuck down and he held me tightly. Rebecca was sick as fuck. Hearing him say Syd was his daughter cut deep as hell and that's some shit that I'll take to the grave. There was no fuckin' way my father needed to know that, and I couldn't risk anyone else spilling that to him so that shitty version of the story died with Gato. I didn't even have to say that shit to Giz because he already knew.

After I got myself together, I gave Gizmo his gun back and he stayed behind waiting for the cleaners, as I made my way back to my party. I slipped back in and everyone was so turnt up they hadn't even realized I'd stepped out. I jumped right back into the festivities because I had more reasons than one to celebrate. Tonight was heavy, but I could move forward in peace and nothing compared to that. We were completely free!

Messiah

I opted out of having a bachelor party. Instead, I went to the park that I normally go to and chilled. I brought a bottle of Glenlivet Scotch that my grandfather bought me as a wedding gift and an ounce of weed with me. I wanted to reflect on life and have a moment of peace and tranquility. Almost losing my kids and my fiancée had changed me in ways that I never even imagined. I thought after losing Nash my life would never be the same and it wasn't, it was better. I still missed him every single day, but I couldn't allow that pain to win. I had my babies looking up at me and expecting me to be their hero, so that's where I had to focus my energy.

As of two month ago, I gave up selling pills, guns, medical supplies, and everything else I had a hand in. All my illegal dealings were done. I still get a profit, but I'm not directly involved at all. After I made Solo my VP, I passed that torch to him. When I told Jax I was going to give her a happily ever after, I meant that shit whole heartedly and I couldn't do that with the DEA breathing down my neck and niggas lurking in the shadows all the time. We had made it through too much for me to jeopardize our future for greed. I had millions in my accounts from all the legal businesses and even more stashed from the illegal shit. We didn't need or want for shit, so it was time. I hadn't even told her yet, but she knew it was in the works.

I looked down at my phone and smiled at her call coming through. Damn I couldn't wait to marry my best friend tomorrow. "Hey beautiful." I answered her call.

"Hey handsome. Everyone is still partying, but I needed to hear your voice. Can you believe we're actually getting married tomorrow?"

"I can and I'm excited. You not gettin' cold feet on me, are you?"

"Not in a million fuckin' years, Daddy. I couldn't imagine my life without you, and I can't wait to proudly become Mrs. Knight. I just mean we've been through hell and back and now our happiness seems so reachable that it's scary. For so long we were fueled by revenge and determined to avenge our people that we lost sight of everything else. Now we're happy and I'm scared that--"

"Don't be scared of shit, baby. Nothing at all. We've had a year of highs and I want you to get used to those because we're only going higher from here. You have so many clients now that you're on track to expand your business. Your mother is healthy and the relationship between you two is better than it's ever been. You probably talk to her ass more than you talk to me." She laughed because Kabrina was an amazing woman and she'd proved that to Jax every chance she got. Her and Brian moved in together and then Alyssa moved in with them so they could help her with the baby. Her baby daddy is fully involved in their son's life, but as a new mother she wanted to be home with help. Carmine just moved out here to be closer to her and the baby, so they'll probably be moving soon.

Kabrina stepped all the way up for Jax but also Brian's other four children, and everyone loved her including me. "We take trips once sometimes twice a month, we have a beautiful home, family that loves unconditionally, and most importantly we have each other and all three of our babies who smile and giggle more than anything else Ma. We're blessed and nothing is going to change that. This is what I promised you so accept it and get comfortable because this is just the beginning."

"It's only one issue with what you just said."

My face scrunched up. "What's the issue?"

"It's no longer three babies."

"Don't play with me, Jaxsyn."

"I wouldn't. I know how much you've been wanting a baby and I know you were pissed when I told you I was still taking birth control, so I stopped. I said if it happens it happens and it happened. I'm five weeks, Baby."

"You have no idea how happy you just made me, Tink."

"I might have a slight idea." I turned around and she was walking up. I stood and damn near ran to her. I scooped her into my arms and swung her around.

"Why you smell like alcohol if you're pregnant with my baby."

"We made a toast, but I only sipped it." She took my face into her hands. "Tonight has been everything, and I know you needed this time to yourself and I'm not staying long, but it wouldn't be complete if I didn't hear your voice, see your face, or touch you."

"My Tink." I pulled her closer and pecked her lips.

"I'm so addicted to you." She stroked the side of my face like I do to her. "Make love to me baby." She said seductively, making a nigga brick up.

I slowly started to undress her and then picked her up as I stared deeply into her eyes. Life tried to shit on us but our love for each other wouldn't allow it to happen. I remember telling my brother what I wanted in a woman right after I broke up with Mariah. He laughed and told me *good luck finding a unicorn in Detroit* and we joked around about it. A couple weeks later I met Jax, and I be damn if she wasn't my fuckin' unicorn. She came into my life and showed me a love that I didn't even know existed.

I slid inside of her and watched pleasure wash over her whole existence. Her head fell back and then to the side making her hair sexily fall to her shoulder. Her hair had grown back from where they operated, and she was wearing it down again which I loved.

"Shit baby." She rolled her hips. My hands curved her ass and I started bouncing her up and down. She was leaking like a faucet and I knew she had to get back to the hotel but after all that good shit she showed up talkin', I had to lay this dick down and show her what got her ass addicted in the first place. Damn I can't wait to give her my last name.

Zionna

Last night was wild as hell and when I woke up, I ran straight to the bathroom throwing up. I was so weak I had to lay out on the floor in the bathroom. I welcomed the cold tile and laid there for what seemed like an hour. Eventually Fresh came to the bathroom door and busted out laughing.

"This what yo' ass get, man. Stop fuckin' playing with me, Z."

"Not right now Londre. I'm not in the damn mood for your shenanigans."

"Shenanigans? Get yo' pregnant ass up and take this test. I don't think you want to talk about shenanigans with me Zionna." He leaned up against the door. "You gon' take yo' ass to that fuckin' bachelorette party knowing damn well you're carrying my baby, so you deserve everything my lil nigga puttin' you through right now."

"I said I'm not in the mood." I slowly pulled myself away from the cold tile and stood up slowly. I bent over at the sink to brush my teeth and Fresh watched me the whole time. I wanted a baby, and I knew that's where I was in my life. I was more than ready, but I was terrified. I had a baby by his cousin and now I'm pregnant by him. Granted, everyone loved us together and even Sih's ass had come around completely, I just didn't know how to feel other than scared.

"How many drinks did you have?"

"A half of a drink, if that. There was so much shit going on I didn't want more than that. I was watching everything that was going on. MGM was going crazy last night for Jaxsyn. I didn't even know she knew that many people." I laughed but it was the truth. Half-naked men and women were everywhere and doing everything. She had the whole hood in that bitch spending big money on drinks and gambling like we were in Vegas. When we finally made it upstairs to the rooms, everybody on the floor was her people so all the doors were propped open, and the shit was crazy. Messiah end up showing up towards the end and he had his Knights with him, so shit went from calming down to getting started all over again.

"Take this test Zionna or admit that you're pregnant. Why the fuck you so in denial about this shit? You're pregnant! I told you I could feel it a month ago. You're gaining weight, it's all in your face, and look at ya' fuckin' stomach ma." He came up behind me and placed his hands on my stomach as he stared at me through the mirror. God I loved this man. I was so grateful for him. He bent down and started kissing me on my neck. When he made it to my collar bone chills crept down my spine. "Tell me daddy's baby is in here Ma."

"Mmm." I moaned as one of his hands slid down my stomach, into my panties, and across my clit. His sexy ass knew exactly what he was doing. "Daddy's baby is in here." I looked at him through the mirror and he smirked. Everything about this moment and this man was perfect.

"I'm the happiest fuckin' man on the planet, Pretty Girl. I love you so much."

"I love you too, Londre Knight." I turned around and we stared at each other before he placed me on the bathroom sink. Our love filled the space we were in and a smile spread across both of our faces. This was happiness in its purest form.

When we first became serious, he promised that all my days with him would be memorable no matter what, and he's definitely fulfilled that promise. I wake up to breakfast in bed daily, he caters to my every need and want, makes the sweetest love to me, and when I look into his eyes, I see nothing but love. He was my blessing and just that quick he put my mind at ease about the baby.

"Thank you."

"Anything for you, Daddy."

"Dead ass? So, you gon' give me another baby after this one?" He slid my panties to the side, and I tucked the corner of my lip under my teeth. I couldn't wait to feel him inside of me.

"Anything but that Boo Boo." We both busted out laughing hysterically. This was us. Always laughing, joking, and enjoying our life together. He was my second chance and without his love I don't even want to think about where I would be. In so many ways he saved me from myself and for that, he'll always have my unwavering love.

Jaxsyn

Today was the day! Today was the day I walk down the aisle to pledge my love and loyalty to my best friend and I was beyond excited. I couldn't even sleep. I didn't expect Messiah to show his sexy ass up at MGM last night but when he did, it was on and poppin'. I hadn't gotten enough of him in the park, and I needed him inside of me again. I allowed him to party for about thirty minutes before I pulled him into my room, locked the door, and showed the fuck out. No love making, no stolen kisses, no gazing into his eyes. I fucked the shit out of my future husband. I had him moaning and groaning more than ever before. The best part, that was just the teaser. Tonight, Mrs. Knight is going to show him that he thought he won but he had no fuckin' clue just how much.

"Something old." My mother walked up behind me as I sat at the vanity table in my guest bedroom. I had the whole room set up for my bridal party, equipped with everything we could possibly need. I planned this day down to its very last second. I wanted everything to be as perfect as it could possibly be. When I married Black, I was fuckin' shaking with fear before, during, and after. I questioned my decision a million times before we made it to the courthouse. I knew I wanted to be with him forever, but marriage didn't seem like the right step at the moment. There was so much doubt weighing on me that first time, that was nowhere in sight this time around. This love hit different.

I go to sleep thinking about Messiah and our kids, dream about them, wake up and obsess over them. I'm in love with my family. I watch my man play with our children and my stomach flutters with butterflies. He wakes me up to head, sends me flowers at work damn near every day, full body massages daily, dates at least twice a week, family vacations, romantic vacations, I mean he's on top of everything. I never have to ask for shit because before I can utter the words, he's already doing it. My life was a movie.

"Ma." My eyes glossed over as I stared at a diamond bracelet that I knew her grandmother gave her. It was gorgeous and she's never gotten rid of it.

"I loved your great grandmother more than I loved myself and she gave me this bracelet on the day you were born. She knew how much I adored you before you were even here. She also knew I had been accused of doing drugs and I'm sure she heard the rumors that people whispered behind my back, she still gifted me with this double heart diamond bracelet. No matter how low life took me, I never even came close to selling this bracelet. I wanted to give it to you on your wedding day and I thought I missed my chance, but God had other plans for us." She dabbed my eyes because the tears flowed freely. I prayed for days like this with her. I waited so long for this woman to show up and when she did, she was fuckin' amazing and didn't disappoint at all. I love my mother so fuckin' much it's crazy. This year has been damn good to her and I. We wake up texting each other and its nonstop calls and text throughout the day. I loved every minute of the bond we've built, and I knew she did too.

"Thank you so much! I'll take good care of it. It's absolutely gorgeous." We hugged and she reached behind her again causing everyone in the room to giggle.

"Something New." She passed me a small box. "This is from Messiah." As soon as she said his name I started smiling and everyone hit me with the "awww," causing me to smile even harder. I couldn't even help it.

"I love him so much y'all." I started opening his gift and my mouth dropped open. The ring staring back at me was beautiful and the clarity was insane.

"Wow." Lyss said from the side of me. "Bro plays no games. That rock is serious."

Fresh Start, was engraved on the inside and I took my ring off and slid the new one on. I knew exactly what he meant, and my heart skipped a beat.

"Something borrowed," She passed me another box and Alyssa and Zionna stood up and walked over to me. I gave them a curious look and then opened the box. After staring at it for a moment I broke all the way down. I cried so hard there was no doubt that the makeup artist was going to have to beat my face all over again. They used a part of Sydnee's old jersey and had a garter made out of it. Just so happens her old school colors and my wedding colors, canary yellow and white were the same. They held me and we all cried together. I absolutely loved their creativity and how they included her into my special day. That meant a lot to me. "Alright, last but not least, something blue." She gave me an envelope and when I pulled the picture out, it was the bluest body of water I had ever saw.

"If this nigga bought you an ocean or some shit, I'm Sparta kickin' the fuck out of him out of pure jealousy." Meka, Jagger's wife said, and we all died laughing.

"Turn it around." My mother smiled and when I did, I gasped.

"He bought me a yacht?"

"Your in-laws did." She passed me two blue keys and I started screaming. They had "Lady Knight" painted on the side in my favorite shade of blue and I couldn't believe it. We all started planning dates that we should take it out, laughing and joking about everything, and taking as many pictures as we could. I was on cloud nine already and I hadn't even said "I do" yet.

My dress fit like a glove and that's exactly what I wanted. I didn't want the traditional big puffy dress, I wanted a mermaid dress with an insane train and that's what I got. The top was sheer with Swarovski Crystals embroidered in just the right places for the dress to be sexy but also very elegant. I chose to do a birdcage veil because it matched the style of my dress perfectly. I was flawless from head to toe. We had taken a million pictures and so had our photographer.

"You ready?" My daddy asked as he held his arm out and I intertwined mine.

"More than ready." I looked up at the nights sky as the stars gleamed and glistened, and I wished upon the brightest one. The day had been magical, and I felt like a Queen, so why not… This is why I love you by Major started playing and my daddy kissed the side of my head and we started walking.

I found love in you
And I've learned to love me too
Never have I felt that I could be all that you see
It's like our hearts have intertwined and to the
perfect harmony
This is why I love you
Ooh this is why I love you
Because you love me
You love me
This is why I love you
Ooh this is why I love you
Because you love me
You love me

My eyes landed right on my baby as we turned the corner and started walking down the aisle. The moment his eyes landed on me his cousins started rubbing his shoulders and he shook his head. His eyes never left mine as tears rolled down his face. I couldn't stop my own from escaping my ducts and my dad gently squeezed my hand. My baby bit down on his lip and took a deep breath. To see my man that emotional just at the sight of me damn near brought me to my knees. People had no clue what we had to go through to get to this moment of perfect peace.

Our ceremony was intimate and personal as if no one else was present but us, which is exactly what we wanted. The moon shined off of the lake adding that familiar ambiance of our favorite park, making our night even more magical. For our vows we opted to speak directly from our hearts while we were right in the moment. I don't think there was a dry eye present, including ours. We basked in our love for each other, and everybody witnessed true love firsthand.

I had my ladies to carry a picture of Sydnee down the aisle with them and Messiah's groomsman carried a picture of Nashon. This day wouldn't have been complete without their presence since everyone that we loved was present. The only person missing was Charlene. She still hadn't reached out to Messiah, but he was okay. He simply said he wasn't carrying her burdens and I understood him completely.

My baby's a rider, a fighter, she is my Queen
Nobody can compare to the type of heart that my woman brings
Listen, because you're perfect how you are the way that God made you (perfect)
And you're the only one that I ever wanna wake up to, oh baby
Look how you shining
Girl you a diamond
You know you're priceless (you are)
You know you got that slow glow
I see your halo
In case you don't know, oh-oh

You may not think that you are perfect
Your lips, your eyes, your thighs

Does something to me
But girl I'm telling you you're perfect
Your skin, your curves, your smile
That's on everything
And you ain't gotta have your hair did
Your nails done, no makeup on
Ooh, girl I'm telling you you're perfect
Girl, you're so damn perfect
You're perfect for me

My baby started singing Johnny Gill and Ralph Tresvant *Perfect* to me and I couldn't stop smiling from my soul. This was our song. He used to sing this to me on my bad days, when I was in the hospital. I had plenty of those and he always found a way to cheer me up, signing to me was one of his ways. I watched my husband dance in front of me while singing our song and my heart felt like it was going to leap out of my chest. I married my best friend and wanted to scream. At one point we didn't even know what the next second of our lives would hit us with, but now, that life was a distant memory. We cram so much love and happiness in our days that as long as we have our "now", our past doesn't even matter.

"Yassss Sih! You better love on my sister!" Zionna yelled out as her and Alyssa high fived each other causing me to laugh hysterically at their crazy asses. My baby continued to sing to me, and I wrapped my arms around his neck. His cologne drew me in close and I ran my fingers through his braids as I rolled my hips. We danced in sync and I could feel myself getting wetter by the second. I couldn't wait to show out for my *husband*. One of his hands rested on my butt while the other wrapped around my waist bringing me in closer.

"I love you so fuckin' much, Mrs. Knight." He whispered against my neck, sending chills down my spine.

"I love you too, Mr. Knight."

"How much?" He stared into my eyes and gave me butterflies.

"More than my next breath, Handsome." I leaned my head further back as he came down to kiss me. His kisses seemed more sensual today and I couldn't get enough of them. We hadn't left the dance floor since we arrived at the reception. We hadn't taken a bite of food, or even cut the cake yet. We were floating and it felt damn good.

"Aye, let me get y'all attention real quick." Sih grabbed my hand and we walked over to our family after our song went off. He was tipsy because they made sure they kept a glass in his hand. His hooded eyes had my folds saturated, and I bit down on my bottom lip. "My wife's giving me that look so we about to cut that cake, head out of here, and get this honeymoon poppin', but I wanted to take a moment to just thank everyone at this table."

"*We* want to thank everyone at this table." He nodded as I wrapped my arms around him. We looked at each other for a minute and then turned to everyone we loved the most in this world, and my cup ran over with pure joy. My eyes landed on my parents who were hugged up like teenagers and my heart could barely handle it. Mauricio and Destiny were sitting next to them holding Junior and Nevaeh while smiling up at us with pure love in their eyes which matched Sih's grandparents' expressions. Alyssa had her son Carter on her lap as her head rested on Carmine's shoulder. He was holding Jeniah as she played on his phone. My baby loves her "Untle" and don't play about him at all. They argue all day and have everybody crackin' up. "A year ago, I didn't know if I would walk, talk, or hold my babies again. A year ago, life had our backs up against the ropes, swinging at an invisible opponent. A year ago, we all came together and stood ten toes down for each other. The people at this table risked it all for us. This table of people is home for us."

233

"We can never repay y'all or fully express how much each and every one of you mean to us, but just know we are forever grateful." Sih raised his glass, and I grabbed my water.

"Wait a minute, you're drinking water? You pregnant sis?" Alyssa's loud-mouth ass said, and everyone looked at me for an answer. I swear her being with Carmine has her ass saying and doing all kinds of hood shit. Gone was my little, meek, mild sister. She had become his rider and it wasn't a bad look until times like this one.

"Yes, we're pregnant, heffa." Everyone started to cheer when Z spoke up.

"We are too!" I looked up at Sih and we both smiled. He had come to terms with Fresh and Zionna, of course with a nudge from me but he got there and actually loved them together.

"Congrats! We're so happy for y'all. Fresh you better put a ring on my sisters' finger."

"I plan to." He dropped to one knee like I told him he could do when he asked three months ago if he could propose at the reception. I knew how deep their love was and I've been going crazy holding this secret for this amount of time. She covered her face, and he moved her hands but before he could even say anything, she screamed *yes* so loud that we fell all over each other crackin' up. He just put the ring on her finger and shook his head, making us all laugh again. I swear I love them together and he brings something magical out of her. This day was sheer perfection, and I couldn't have asked for more.

"To us," We raised our glasses. "We've been through hell, but heaven was on our side!" We all cheered, yelled, screamed, and celebrated each other. Life tried to come at us all in so many different ways, but together, we came out on top.

I couldn't have asked for a happier ever after!

THE END...

SPECIAL THANKS

Thank you all so much for the love and support that each of you continuously show me. As a new Author, I was terrified that this gritty series by an unknown name would not have been received so well, but you all showed up and showed out for me.
Forever and always grateful!
This just the beginning.